Ashantee

Studies in Austrian Literature, Culture, and Thought

Translation Series

General Editors:

Jorun B. Johns
Richard H. Lawson

Peter Altenberg

Ashantee

Introduction
by
Wolfgang Nehring

Translated and with an
Afterword and Bibliography
by
Katharina von Hammerstein

Ariadne Press
Riverside, California

Ariadne Press would like to express its appreciation to the Bundesministerium für Unterricht, Kunst und Kultur for assistance in publishing this book.

.KUNST

Translated from the German *Ashantee*
© 1897 and 1904, S. Fischer, Berlin
Illustrations with kind permission of Dokumentationsstelle, Literaturhaus, Vienna, Wien Museum and Österreichische Nationalbliothek, Vienna, Austria

Library of Congress Cataloging-in-Publication Data

Altenberg, Peter, 1859-1919.
　　[Ashantee. English]
　　Ashantee / Peter Altenberg ; translated and with an afterword and bibliography by Katharina von Hammerstein ; introduction by Wolfgang Nehring
　　　　p.　cm. -- (Studies in Austrian literature, culture, and thought. Translation series)
Impressionistic observations (sketches) concerning an ethnographic exhibit of an African village (including its inhabitants) in Vienna in the 1880s.
Includes bibliographical references.
ISBN 978-1-57241-155-5 (alk. Paper)
1.　Ashanti (African people)—Fiction. I. Von Hammerstein, Katharina. II. Title

PT2601.L78A813 2007
830.896'3385--dc22

　　　　　　　　　　　　　　　　　　　　　　2007033951

Cover Design
Art Director: George McGinnis

Fig. 1: Original book cover: Peter Altenberg.
Ashantee. Berlin: Fischer, 1897.

(Dokumentationsstelle, Literaturhaus, Vienna).

Contents

Fig. 2: Peter Altenberg in the Café Central, Herrengasse, Vienna, 1907 (Peter Altenberg's photo collection, Wien Museum, Vienna).

Introduction
by
Wolfgang Nehring

Peter Altenberg and His Time

The Viennese fin de siècle was, from today's point of view, a fascinating period. At no time in modern history was Vienna richer in talent than in the last decade of the nineteenth century and in the beginning of the twentieth – not only in culture and literature but also in science, psychology, and sociopolitics. The names of such luminaries as composers Gustav Mahler and Arnold Schoenberg, painters Gustav Klimt and Egon Schiele, and authors Hermann Bahr, Arthur Schnitzler, Hugo von Hofmannsthal and Karl Kraus; of scientists and psychologists Sigmund Freud, Ernst Mach and Otto Weininger, and of the founder of Zionism Theodor Herzl, bear witness to the intellectual brilliance of the era. Politically, however, the situation was different. The aging emperor Franz Joseph complained about the political unrest, the "permanent revolution" in the Habsburg Monarchy.[1] In a way, the fin de siècle marks the finale of the once glorious Austro-Hungarian Empire.

Originally the term fin de siècle referred merely to the chronological end of the century and implied the end of a certain historical, cultural, and intellectual period. In literature and art it is often equated with "decadence," a term that denotes the demise of a stronger, more vital time. "Decadence" was largely used to censure artists and writers.[2] But most of them did not mind. There was in Vienna a strong feeling of artistic awakening and modernity, and modernism and decadence were not considered contradictory by many protagonists; rather, they appeared as two aspects of the same thing. One could almost say that to be decadent meant to be modern or vice versa: to be "modern" you had to be decadent.

Among the poets and writers, the authors of Young Vienna, the literary group around Hermann Bahr (1863-

1934) stood out. The poet Hugo von Hofmannsthal (1874-1929) and the playwright and novelist Arthur Schnitzler (1862-1932) were soon considered the greatest literary talents of their time and have retained or regained their status in today's literary recollection. The young Hofmannsthal fascinated a whole generation of readers and fellow poets with his beautiful verse and his graceful prose. It was said that if he had died at twenty or twenty-five, he would have had the most beautiful biography as a youthful prodigy. But his later works as well, e.g., his poetic libretti for Richard Strauss or the famous Salzburg *Jedermann* (*Everyman*), live on into the present. Schnitzler, considered the poetic chronicler of pre-World War I Vienna, was rediscovered after World War II because of his intellectual kinship with Sigmund Freud. Freud had tremendous respect for the psychological insights of his Viennese contemporary and envied the famous author as a "double" who recognized through poetic intuition or self inspection what he, Freud, had to learn through serious analytical work.[3] Many other authors, such as the elegant Richard Beer-Hofmann, the versatile Felix Salten, or the struggling Leopold von Andrian, also contributed to the new Vienna and the Austrian scene that Hermann Bahr wished to establish in competition with the activities in the German capital, Berlin.

The poet Peter Altenberg (born Richard Engländer; 1859-1919) had a special status in fin-de-siècle Vienna. He did not belong to any particular literary group or movement. He was an outsider, yet praised by almost everybody – including the more famous or representative contemporary authors mentioned above – for his distinct way and for his highly individual style. His friends, one could say, his fan club, went further: they considered him the greatest Austrian poet of his time or even the greatest Austrian poet since Walther von der Vogelweide, who lived around 1200.[4] The cabaret performer and important cultural historian Egon Friedell wrote an early book about him with the proud title *Ecce Poeta* (1912)[5] – not shying away from reference to Pilate's words regarding Jesus Christ or Friedrich Nietzsche's autobiographical work *Ecce Homo* – in which he portrayed Altenberg as the quintessence of poetic spirit. Soon after P.A. (as he called himself and was referred to by many) died, Friedell collected literary and biographical documents about him and published another volume, his *Altenbergbuch* (*Altenberg Book*; 1922). The writer Alfred Polgar lost himself in wild metaphors when he paid tribute to Altenberg; he told his readers that in his "cataracts of fury and enthusiasm" P.A. had "raged essays, improvised extemporaneously drama, and lived lyric poetry."[6] Even Karl Kraus, whose reputation as an uncompromising and incorruptible critic was well established, believed that Altenberg was not only the "free-est spirit of his epoch" but also the "richest poetic talent in modern Germany."[7] "One sentence of Peter Altenberg," he claimed in 1913, "makes up for an entire Viennese novel."[8] Some compared P.A. with Socrates, some with the famous miracle doctor Paracelsus, others at the very least with Walt Whitman. – When the city of Vienna provided an honorary grave site for the seemingly impoverished author but "forgot" to finance a tombstone as well, Karl Kraus started a campaign to create a dignified resting place for his late friend.

At least four people claimed or were credited with the discovery of Altenberg's literary talent. Arthur Schnitzler, who knew P.A. (or at that time still Richard Engländer) as a previous suitor of Olga Waissnix, Schnitzler's first significant love, met Altenberg in Vienna's Café Central scribbling some sketches and found encouraging words for the prose of his competitor.[9] Karl Kraus makes similar claims and says that he referred P.A. to the leading modern publisher of that time, Samuel Fischer in Berlin.[10] Fritz Eckstein, the owner of a parchment factory and regular guest in Café Griensteidl, where Viennese artists and writers met, is supposed to be the first person who praised

Altenberg's writings enthusiastically.[11] Finally, there is Hedwig Fischer, the publisher's wife, who called P.A. her own discovery. She was so touched by his poetic prose that she convinced her husband to accept his manuscripts.[12] Theirs became a lifelong liaison. Between 1896 and 1919 Fischer published twelve books by Peter Altenberg and in 1925 a posthumous collection. Soon afterwards the author fell more or less into oblivion, and, although numerous scholars and readers regret that he has joined the ranks of "neglected writers," and although several studies and anthologies have been published, there has not yet been an "Altenberg renaissance."

Altenberg's greatest success was his first volume *Wie ich es sehe (How I See It)* of 1896. This book took everybody by surprise; it is a sizable volume of short stories, or rather, the very shortest of stories, sketches, or prose poems. Hugo von Hofmannsthal, Hermann Bahr, and many others wrote glowing reviews of the book, calling it "un-German", i.e., very "Viennese" in its playfulness, gracefulness, in its indifference toward big issues and serious problems. They were fascinated by the poetry of everyday life in these writings, by the author's love of common people, particularly children and very young women, by his untroubled conscience in digressing into elaborate descriptions of clothes, gestures, atmospheric details, trivialities of all kinds; they admired the refined, coquettish simplicity and charm, and they found in it the "freedom of artistic culture."[13] Hermann Bahr, who sometimes inclined toward the pompous, saw in the book a "treasure chest" of the past, through which the author directs us to a "new Austria."[14]

Nothing could be further from the truth. Peter Altenberg was intrigued by the present and had no ambitions whatever to strive for a great Austrian future. The content and style of his later books have no wider outlook and are quite similar to those of his first. His second volume, *Ashantee*, from 1897, rendered here for the first time in English, is in a way an exception among Altenberg's works because it concentrates on a very specific topic, a very specific group of people; but as in his other works P.A. approaches these people with subjective enthusiasm and condenses his observations into miniature poetic sketches. *Was der Tag mir zuträgt (What the Day Brings Me)*, which followed in 1901, is almost a sequel to *Wie ich es sehe*. One volume is called *Märchen des Lebens (Fairy Tale of Life*; 1908), and Thomas Mann rightfully observed that this title could be applied to the author's complete oeuvre.[15] Some readers were taken aback by *Prodromos* (1906) when questions of diet and hygiene received major attention for the first (but not the last) time, and the author felt called upon to advise his readers on perfumes, laxatives, weight loss, and other health issues. Yet his friends and defenders gave him credit for being a reformer and did not feel in the least disturbed by such content nor did their poetic appreciation diminish.

Contemporaries report that P.A. wrote his works quite casually in cafés. Poetry came to him naturally. For him, seeing, loving, and writing were all organic activities. A true poet could not do anything else. He wished to have these words inscribed on his tombstone: "He loved and he saw."[16] His seeing, however, was not limited to eyesight. He observed reality with all his senses and nerves. He saw, heard, smelled, tasted, and felt it. In things that appear dull or insignificant to others, he discovered a sparkling poetic life. Kafka called Altenberg a "genius of trivialities" and a "strange idealist."[17] "Life" was the key word of the epoch, the highest value that all wished to rally behind. But in P.A.'s stories life does not appear in Nietzschean grandeur, Dionysian passion or spectacular action, but rather in subtleties of everyday dreams and relationships. For the most part his tales don't even have a plot. He compared his writings to pocket mirrors, which are not intended to reflect the entire world. In a rare self-critical remark he wrote that while many considered his writings to be merely "small samples," "this is all I can do."[18] At the same time he was very proud that he had found the ideal form for a hectic epoch which had no time for long novels. His pieces may be short, but he considered them true "extracts" of reality. Friedell called him admiringly the "only consistent impressionist" of the period.[19] The novelist Thomas Mann, by contrast, controlled his admiration and expressed grudges. He did not appreciate that Altenberg tried to make a doctrine out of his personal manner; Mann, who planned his works in advance with extreme care, also had considerable doubts about the sincerity of P.A.'s claim of writing spontaneously.[20]

And here we come to the problem of Peter Altenberg's "existence." P.A. was not only a charming writer but also a mythical figure; he embodied a myth which one could embrace, could believe – or not. Was he the "free-est spirit", as we have heard, or a poseur? Altenberg's personality (or the legend of his personality) became an integral part of his reception. After his early success his eccentric character contributed a great deal to public interest in his work. He knew this and cultivated his image. For many his posture appears to have been the larger part of his attraction. This may partly explain why his works lost their resonance so soon after his death. Some readers enjoyed his writings and admired their magic *in spite* of the author's alienating extravagance, others looked at his works mostly *because* of his eccentricity.

What is the Peter Altenberg myth about? What made P.A.'s personality so unusual? Born into a well-to-do merchant family during a very bourgeois age, he became a bohemian. After some unsuccessful academic attempts in law and medicine and a short exposure to book selling he was diagnosed by a physician as hyper-sensitive and incapable of pursuing any profession or systematic occupation. This diagnosis was quite convenient; it enabled Altenberg to continue his carefree life and to follow his personal inclinations: courting women, traveling to the countryside, reading, writing, drinking ... – at least as long as the family business remained in good shape and his father and brother supported him. Thereafter he found other means of subsistence in addition to writing and occasional journalistic work. He went into fund raising among friends and acquaintances, in Vienna as well as in Germany. He convinced writers, critics, professionals, aesthetic circles of men and women that they could not allow a poet like himself to go under. Hofmannsthal, Schnitzler, Kraus, the architect Adolf Loos, and many others were approached for regular support and generously contributed to his maintenance. In Germany the critic Alfred Kerr started two financial campaigns on his behalf;[21] Samuel Fischer and his wife donated extensively. – There are many anecdotes about P.A.'s need of money and lavish spending habits. Hofmannsthal relates[22] how at an assembly of would-be helpers, Lina Loos, the wife of the architect, claimed she loved and understood P.A. better than anybody else. She felt that it would be most decent and dignified to let him die peacefully. Altenberg, who had been sitting in the background, sick, seemingly indifferent, and resigned to a grim fate, jumped forward furiously and shouted, "Stupid goose, I don't want to die, I want to live." He desired good food and champagne, he demanded a "warm room with a gas heater and an American rocking chair ..." and most of all a "pension." Apparently, when Peter Altenberg died, he had 100.000 crowns in his savings account, which he left to a children's fund.

After P.A. moved out of his family home in 1886 he no longer had a place of his own. He lived in a small hotel room, which he decorated with postcards and hundreds of well-framed photographs of beautiful women, many of them in the nude. In his autobiographical note in *What the Day Brings Me* he states: "There is only one indecent attitude toward nudity ... to find nudity indecent."[23] He slept during the day and went to cafés and nightclubs at night. He was the center of attention wherever he went, partly for his unusual looks – bald head, big moustache, colorful checked shirts, heavy jacket or pelerine, in his early years gaiters, later often just wooden sandals – and partly for his behavior: wild speeches or melancholy observations. Surrounded by fans and friends who were watching out for his excesses, he appeared extraordinary and a little pathological. He was admired as much as smiled at. People sought him out to flirt with the unconventional, to escape from normality. And for this pleasure they maintained him.

Altenberg's friend Karl Kraus found this attitude exploitive and blasphemous. He did not like Egon Friedell imitating P.A. in cabaret style, telling real or invented anecdotes about him,[24] although P.A. himself mostly enjoyed this. Kraus also disliked Hermann Bahr's pathetic praise because he thought that Bahr was a phony. Admirers of Peter Altenberg were often not each others' friends! At no time did Kraus accept the notion that P.A. might be a poseur. He loved him because he considered him the only sincere character or poet in the literary scene of Vienna. Perhaps he loved him because he detested most others, as Altenberg himself suggests in *Vita ipsa* (1918).[25] But even Kraus could not overlook Altenberg's bizarreness, his rapidly changing positions, his contradictions, and his unreliability. He decided that the poet hid himself under a magic hat or behind a mask to camouflage his inner self – an explanation that unintentionally attains the opposite of its aim and supports doubts in the truthfulness of Altenberg's style. Actors or sorcerers are not the best guarantors of genuineness. Altenberg himself proposes a different explanation of his personality. In *Mein Lebensabend* (*Dusk of My Life;* 1919) he claims to be devoid of all prejudice.[26] He does not, he implies, have to care about tradition, history, conventions, prescribed behavior, or any of the "common lies of life." He just wishes to be P.A., as he says in *What the Day Brings Me*: "I was nothing, I am nothing, I'll be nothing. But I live my life in full freedom" and allow others to participate in "my free soul ... I am poor, but I am myself! Completely myself. The man who does not make concessions."[27] Not making concessions includes freedom from the law of time. Life begins every day anew; there is no need to be bound by the past, by previous days and their obligations. This is impressionistic; it is part of what Friedell had in mind when he called P.A. the "most consistent impressionist."

Altenberg's unconventional life had drawbacks. We have seen that he tried to assume the role of a health reformer who freely advised people on their life style. In his own life, however, this did not work out. He became a heavy drinker, who could sleep only with strong sleeping medications or after consuming batteries of beer or great amounts of wine. In the end, his irregular, strenuous and unhealthy life style destroyed his already weak nervous system. He squandered not only money, but also his other material assets. For years friends had financed stays in nature resorts or health spas. In 1909 he had to enter a special water clinic, and in the following years he was transferred to various psychiatric institutions, one of them the *Steinhof*, the most notorious asylum of Vienna. Arthur Schnitzler, himself a physician with an interest in psychiatry, visited P.A. there and did not find him any more insane than before. He helped him to get released, but in spite of a vacation on the Lido of Venice, accompanied by his faithful friends Adolf Loos and Karl Kraus, P.A.'s nerves and physical condition remained extremely shaky.

The most important experience in Altenberg's life as well as in his writings was his love for women. He was not driven by sexual desire, but rather by the wish to understand their souls, admire their beautiful bodies, and demonstrate his devotion to them. He says in an early letter to Schnitzler that the lack of sexual prowess can be compensated by the refinement of psychological powers.[28]

Since he felt that this was so in his case, the objects of his devotion could be very young women, girls in whom he discovered the first signs of womanhood. He fell for girls, elegant ladies, and simple service women. In all of them, he insisted, a goddess resided or had once resided. Many observers note that P.A. seemed to have the soul of a woman. He saw his role as that of a troubadour, singing the praise of women without hope for personal gratification. In an autobiographical sketch a male skeptic asks the poet: "You venerate women, but you don't take possession of them – what do you get out of it?" P.A.'s answer: "You take possession of them, but don't venerate them – what do you get out of that?"[29] Peter Altenberg wished to explain to the overworked and insensitive male the "lovely, tender, mysterious creature" next to him.[30] Men, after all, are dull sexual predators, he thought. Since he thought himself the only one who completely understood women's desires and needs, he felt that he had to inform the male-dominated world about the female. Men had to be taught to become more "ideal" and "godlike" so that they might care for the true wishes of womankind.

There were always women in Altenberg's personal life whom he loved "fanatically." This word is one of his hallmarks – for him it was neither unpoetic nor disagreeable but rather expressed the highest intensity of his feeling. Every love of his was the first and "unique," a non-plus-ultra, and he could assume any role in it. For the young actress Anni Mewes, his last love, the fifty-seven year-old poet wished to be father, brother, lover, courtier, husband in one person.[31] Sometimes he spoke of motherly feelings as well. Mostly his sensual yet platonic love affairs – full of new or rather old (Petrarchan) imagery, erotic dreams, and bold wishes – did not get off the ground, but a great number of women nonetheless enjoyed his enthusiasm and accepted his quixotic devotion gracefully. When he was in the psychiatric clinics he had many caring visitors.

When Altenberg was interested in a woman, he became jealous of any man who talked with her. He could call his best friend a "cowardly envious enemy" and terminate their friendship "for eternity" – until some time had passed and the unworthy felon once again became his closest friend, the "only man in the world" who was not a "crazy, cowardly, criminal idiot."[32] When Adolf Loos was about to marry Lina, Altenberg tried to undermine the relationship by calling Loos a coward who was only afraid of losing his lust-object; he portrayed him in letters to Lina as one of these sexual vultures to whom nothing is "holy" or a "work of art."[33] – But most astounding is that in personal situations, when Altenberg's own wishes were at stake or when he wanted to "rescue" a male friend, he could slip out of his troubadour mode and warn his friend of the fateful disaster called "woman" or "bitch." For example, he tried to convince Egon Friedell that he was endangered and should not believe in "vain, stupid, cowardly impudent" women; he should rather stick to his alcohol, because being drunk meant escape from the petty and worthless side of life.[34] A "dirty whore" without soul, spirit, charm, or talent should not steal his friend from him. Adolf Loos said that those who knew only Altenberg's books were shocked when they heard him speak about women in reality because "he knew" them,[35] and Lina Loos expressed the opinion that the supposed admirer of womankind in reality hated women because they wasted their best gifts on the wrong people and passed him by.[36]

Most people in P.A.'s inner circle ("soul circle" as Hofmannsthal and others mockingly called it) took his outbursts and unjust insults in stride. They were so fascinated by his inner riches and personal charisma that they did not question his principal goodness. The some-time "cowards," "criminals," "murderers" remained loyal friends in good and bad times. More circumspect obser-vers such as Arthur Schnitzler distanced themselves from

P.A.'s untrustworthy character – shocked by incidents like the following: A young man had fallen in love with Lina Loos and had been rejected. When the unhappy youth asked Peter Altenberg what he should do, the author advised him that a true lover would kill himself, but since he was a coward like everybody else he certainly would continue to live. Thereupon, the young man shot himself.[37] Schnitzler started to write his tragicomedy *Das Wort* (*The Word*) on the basis of this story, exposing the decadent writer and his irresponsible use of words. Yet this work remained a fragment because Schnitzler could not reconcile in one dramatic character his admiration for Altenberg's poetic spirit and his disgust with his vanity and unreliability.

Peter Altenberg had threatened the world innumerable times with his impending doom, had informed his brother, friends and devotees, anybody who might care, that he was close to dying. Whenever he needed support, a favor, or just attention, he announced that he was as good as lost. There always appeared to be some truth to his statements because he was indeed a sick man. But were these alarms really serious? Did he himself believe in them? At least it seems that he did not mind his frail condition; he felt that through sickness he obtained a deeper understanding of the human condition, and as a sick person he also wielded power over others, over the healthy ones. In any case, he did not do much to improve his health! Was he playing the death card in anticipation of an early demise? Perhaps it was more of a safeguard; perhaps he talked so much about dying in an attempt to keep the reality of death at bay. In his final year, people had no doubts that he was really very sick and helpless. He considered himself a "living dead body," but nonetheless kept his humor, proud and unsentimental in his decline. He made plans for his 60th birthday and expected others to make them. But Altenberg died before he reached this goal. Karl Kraus gave the memorial speech at his grave and concluded with Goethe's famous words from *Götz von Berlichingen*: "Woe to the age that rejected you; woe to a posterity that fails to recognize you!"[38]

Notes

All German-language quotes were translated by Wolfgang Nehring.

[1] Klaus Hildebrandt, "Was das 19. Jahrhundert alles brachte," Lothar Gall (ed.), *Das Jahrtausend im Spiegel der Jahrhundertwenden*, Berlin: Propyläen, 1999, 345.

[2] See particularly Max Nordau, *Entartung* (*Degeneration*), 2 vols., Berlin: Duncker, no year (1892/93).

[3] Sigmund Freud, "Briefe an Arthur Schnitzler" ("Letters to Arthur Schnitzler"), *Neue Rundschau* 66 (1955): 95-106.

[4] Egon Friedell (ed.), *Das Altenbergbuch*, Leipzig/Wien: Wiener Graphische Werkstätte, 1922, 310.

[5] Egon Friedell, *Ecce Poeta,* Zürich: Diogenes, 1992.

[6] Alfred Polgar, "Wirkung der Persönlichkeit," Friedell (ed.), *Das Altenbergbuch* (note 4), 265.

[7] Karl Kraus, *Die Fackel* 806 (1929): 12 and 16.

[8] Karl Kraus, *Die Fackel* 374 (1913): 16.

[9] Kurt Bergel (ed.), Arthur Schnitzler. *Das Wort,* Frankfurt am Main: Fischer, 1966, p. 8.

[10] Peter Altenberg, "Wie ich mir Karl Kraus gewann," *Vita ipsa,* Berlin: S. Fischer, 1918, 165-167.

[11] Stefan Grossmann, in: Christian Kosler (ed.), *Peter Altenberg: Leben und Werk in Texten und Bildern,* München: Matthes & Seitz, 1981, 116.

[12] Hedwig Fischer, cf. Kosler (ed.) (note 11), p. 244.

[13] Hugo von Hofmannsthal, "Ein neues Wiener Buch," *Gesammelte Werke, Reden und Aufsätze I*, Bernd Schoeller (ed.), Frankfurt/M.: Fischer, 1979, 222-230.

[14] Hermann Bahr, "Ein neuer Dichter," Gotthart Wunberg (ed.), *Das junge Wien. Österreichische Literatur- und Kunstkritik*, 2 vols., vol. 1, Tübingen: Niemeyer, 1976, 589.

[15] Thomas Mann, "Brief über Peter Altenberg," Friedell (ed.). *Das Altenbergbuch* (note 4), 69-77.

[16] Peter Altenberg, "Selbstbiographie," *Was der Tag mir zuträgt*, Berlin: S. Fischer, 7th ed., 1919, p. 8.

[17] Kosler (ed.) (note 11), p. 52.

[18] Peter Altenberg, "Brief an Arthur Schnitzler" (1894), Friedell (ed.). *Das Altenbergbuch* (note 4), 81-83.

[19] Egon Friedell, *Kulturgeschichte der Neuzeit* (first ed. in 3 vols., 1927-31), München: Beck, 1965, 1456.

[20] Thomas Mann (note 15), 73.

[21] In 1904, Kerr used the pseudonym of the Romantic poet Jean Paul for this purpose and was quite successful; his campaign of 1908 was initiated by P.A. himself but did not raise much money.

[22] Hugo von Hofmannsthal, *Gesammelte Werke, Reden und Aufsätze III, Aufzeichnungen*, Bernd Schoeller and Ingeborg Beyer-Ahlert (eds.), Frankfurt/M.: Fischer, 1980, 455-456.

[23] Peter Altenberg, "Selbstbiographie" (note 16), 7.

[24] Karl Kraus, *Die Fackel* 370 (1913): 30; *Die Fackel* 546 (1920): 38.

[25] Peter Altenberg, *Vita ipsa* (note 10), 166.

[26] Peter Altenberg, "Antwort an Egon Friedell," *Mein Lebensabend*, 9th ed., Berlin: S. Fischer, 1919, 143.

[27] Peter Altenberg, "Selbstbiographie" (note 16), 7.

[28] Peter Altenberg, Unpublished letter to Arthur Schnitzler, July 30, 1895, quoted in Bergel (ed.), *Das Wort* (note 9), 8.

[29] Peter Altenberg, "Splitter," *Nachfechsung*, (Berlin: S. Fischer, 1916), *Ausgewählte Werke in zwei Bänden*, vol. 2, München: Hanser, 1979, 65.

[30] Peter Altenberg, "Selbstbiographie" (note 16), 11

[31] Peter Altenberg, "Fünfzehn Briefe an die Schauspielerin Anni Mewes," Friedell (ed.), *Das Altenbergbuch* (note 4), 4.

[32] Peter Altenberg, "Zwölf Briefe an Egon Friedell," Friedell (ed.), *Das Altenbergbuch* (note 4), 325-326.

[33] Peter Altenberg, "Neun Briefe an Frau Lina L.," Friedell (ed.), *Das Altenbergbuch* (note 4), 173 and 181.

[34] Peter Altenberg's letters to Friedell (note 32), 327 and 331.

[35] Adolf Loos, "Abschied von Peter Altenberg" ("Farewell to Peter Altenberg"), Friedell (ed.), *Das Altenbergbuch* (note 4), 366.

[36] Lina Loos, "Peter Altenbergs Fluchtversuche" (*Der Querschnitt* 9, 1929), quoted in Kosler (ed.) (note 11), 108.

[37] This incident is also reported in Hofmannsthal, *Reden und Aufsätze III, Aufzeichnungen* (note 22), 455-457. Hofmannsthal thought of rendering it into a comedy called "Die Seelen" ("The Souls").

[38] Karl Kraus, "Rede am Grabe Peter Altenbergs, 11. Juni 1919" ("Oration at Peter Altenberg's Funeral, June 11, 1919"), *Die Fackel* 508 (1919): 8-25.

24

Ashantee

by

Peter Altenberg

Motto:

"Not unto *yourself* and to only *one* person should you bestow the good that you have found on your difficult journey – – – give it to *everyone*!

Cast off the cowardly caution that keeps you from revealing yourself to *like-minded* souls!

Be strong! *Give it to the world!* And let yourself be crucified!!"

Peter Altenberg

Ashantee

(In the Vienna Zoological Garden with the Negroes
from the Gold Coast, West Coast)

Dedicated
to my Black women friends,
the unforgettable paradise people
Alolé, Akóshia, Tíoko, Djôjô, Nāh-Badûh

MEYER'S ENCYCLOPEDIA.
Volume I, page 900, Ashantee:

"Negro[1] kingdom in Guinea, West Coast, Gold Coast. Forced back from the coast 130 kilometers by the English. Headquarters of the English colony on the coast: Accra.

The soil of the country is mostly light clay. The climate is temperate. Rainy season twice a year, end of May, end of October. Most utilizable trees: palm trees, gum trees. Staple food: yam root (a plant similar to our potato). The Ashantee are full-blooded, authentic, curly-haired Negroes who speak Odschi; they are especially skillful in weaving rugs and making gold jewelry. They practice polygyny. Their religious practice consists of fetishism. The priests' mystical duties lie mainly in appeasing evil spirits through obscure ceremonies and hysterical dances. The capital of Ashantee: Coomassie.

On February 4th, 1874, General Wolseley[2] marched into Coomassie; the King surrendered the entire coastal region and promised to abolish human sacrifice.

See also: Brackenbury, *The Ashantee War*.[3] Stanley, *Coomasie and Magdala*.[4]

---

[1] While the terms Negro or Negro woman may offend present day readers and would today be replaced by "African" or "Black African," they are used here because they reflect the German-language original and late nineteenth-century Austrian and German discourse.

[2] Garnet Joseph Wolseley, 1st Viscount, Baron Wolseley of Cairo and of Wolseley (1833-1913), British field marshal.

[3] Henry Brackenbury. *Narratives of the Ashantee War*. 2 vols. Edinburgh, 1874.

[4] Henry Morton Stanley. *Coomasie and Magdala. The Story of Two British Campaigns in Africa*. London: Sampson Low, Marston & Co., 1891.

Der Häuptling der Aschantis mit seinem Hofstaat.

Fig. 3: "The Chief of the Ashanti and His Court," Ashanti exhibit at the Vienna Zoological Garden, newspaper *Wiener Bilder* II.20 (May 16, 1897): 3 (Austrian National Library, Vienna).

THE TUTOR

Close to the entrance of the Zoological Garden with its black wire fence and dusty lilacs stood a little light brown Swiss chalet gleaming with varnish, roasting in the afternoon sun. Inside sat the zoo keeper dining on a pear. He sold lemon yellow admission tickets and dark green discounted ones for clubs, soldiers and regulars. "Les enfants ne comptent pas (children don't count – or pay)," he used to say, as though dismissing them with a, "Get lost, beat it, you have little significance –   –   – ." Close to the roasting little Swiss chalet two agoutis sat in their cage. They were Dasyprocta Agoutis. The floor of the cage was covered with bread crumbs and lumps of sugar.

A young tutor, accompanying a boy and a girl, said, "Those ignorant people. Agoutis only feed on fruit! Watch." He handed them a little peach.

The Agoutis ate like squirrels sitting on their hind legs. The little girl glowed with admiration for the tutor and sensed that all the others standing nearby respected him in the same way.

"Remind me, Fortunatina, tomorrow I will read to you from Brehm's Encyclopedia about the favorite meals of the Onza ... jaguars ... Brazil. These two are in the prime of life. But bread and sugar?! They are not monkeys, after all."

Then they went on to the bears, which were making their typical movements and smelled terrible. The crowd called to them continuously, urging them to go into their pool.

"Wait," said the tutor, as he threw a whole roll into the pool. Now the bear had to go in, even if only with the front part of its body.

At the cage of the lioness Fortunatina propped her elbows on the wooden barrier and stared for a long time. The lioness crept back and forth, almost gliding over the wet stone floor. She appeared to be stalking something, but what?!

The tutor and the boy stayed further back. The boy was anxious to move on: "A lioness, what's there to see?! She's caged, after all ..."

Quietly, the tutor remained where he was.

"Fortunatina and the lioness – – –," he thought. He didn't know at all what it meant or what meaning it could have. But it felt to him like a ballad which no one had yet composed. The ballad is already conceived and wants to be born; called into life by a poet. In some person's mind it already exists, pressing forward into the light of day, wanting to become a song – – – Fortunatina and the lioness!

The tutor remained standing silently.

The little girl turned around, blushed, smiled in embarrassment and prepared to leave.

"It is not shameful to lose yourself in animals," the tutor thought. Smiling, he placed his wonderful fatherly hands on the child's shoulders.

Fortunatina was dreaming, "– – – suddenly, in the middle of the night, a roaring, powerful enough to make all of nature tremble – – –. One blow with the paw can fell a bull – – –. There are cases of – – – Africa. Africa! In spite of cold-bloodedness and determination fearless hunters have often, in the last moment – – –."

She glanced at the tutor, in his baggy Papita trousers, dark jacket and little brown felt hat. On top of that he held a walking stick with a handle made of antler and wore gold-rimmed eye-glasses. If only he had been standing there clad all in yellow leather! At least in leggings.

They continued their walk.

The sound of iron castanets, hollow wooden drums and brass rings could be heard.

They came to the Ashantee dancing area.

"Syncopated rhythms," said the tutor, "can you hear it?! Tada tadada dada tadada – – –."

"Just like our threshing flails at home," said the boy.

"Quite right," said the tutor, "syncopation."

"Really, just like threshers," said Fortunatina.

"Or like the clattering beneath the floor in a railway carriage," said the boy.

"Really, just like in a railway carriage," said Fortunatina. "One ought to compose music for it with real instruments."

"Bravo, Fortunatina – – –," said the tutor.

"To them it is music, at any rate – – –," said the boy.

"Don't place such an abyss between us and them. To them, to them. What does that mean?! Do you think that way because there are stupid people who act as if they are superior to them, and treat them like exotic animals?! Why?! Because their epidermis consists of dark pigmentation?! These young girls, at any rate, are gentle and good. Come here, little one. What's your name?!"

"Tíoko – – –."

He took her wonderful brown hand and placed it into Fortunatina's hand; Fortunatina became embarrassed.

Then he took a four-stranded string of white glass beads with a golden clasp from his pocket and gave it to Tíoko.

"Where did you get those?!" the boy asked, whereas to Fortunatina that seemed obvious.

"Well, I wonder," replied the tutor.

Later the boy said, "You were nice and gentle with Tíoko, and now you believe she was the same way with you; just the opposite."

The tutor looked at him as if to say, "Silly thing, isn't that the solution to our entire entangled, complicated existence?" Instead he said, "Fortunatina, wasn't Tíoko gentle and kind?! Well, there you go! She came with us like a loyal and trusting creature, and didn't let go of your hand. What pleasure she took in those glass beads. Look at her whole being. This immaculateness, this wonderful smooth, cool skin, these ivory teeth, these delicate hands and feet, this nobility of the joints and limbs!"

The boy thought, "But I'm still right. He just bought her."

"Tíoko, I love you," said Fortunatina at their parting.

The boy thought, "Fortunatina overdramatizes everything."

The tutor kissed Tíoko.

Fortunatina felt, "They are all so gentle: Tíoko, the poor lioness, the tutor. It is just like in paradise, where humans and wild animals − − −."

The boy said, "How much were those glass beads?! How come you had them?! Why won't you tell me?"

"Why do you think?! There is a way to open every person's heart. And you just have to find the key that fits."

The boy thought, "Tíoko is just interested. It is as simple as that."

Fortunatina felt, "I would like to cry, about Tíoko, about the lioness, about everything."

Close to the exit of the garden the two Agoutis were still sitting in their cage. And those ignorant people were still feeding them rolls and lumps of sugar. The zoo keeper was still sitting in the little, light brown lacquered Swiss chalet selling lemon yellow admission tickets and dark green discounted ones for clubs, soldiers and regular customers.

"Are you tired, Fortunatina?!" the tutor asked.

"A little − − −."

"Let's sit down then − − −."

In a grove, surrounded by meadows and a few stands of trees, there was a bench. They all sensed the pleasant silence and huddled together, so to speak. From his pocket the tutor took a four-stranded string of white glass beads with a golden clasp and placed it around Fortunatina's neck.

She trembled with the joy of paradise.

They were all silent.

The boy was embarrassed.

"A sweet perfume is drifting in from the meadows –," said the tutor.

They all deeply inhaled the fragrant breeze Mother Earth exhaled from her wonderful lungs, or rather from her pores

"What is Tíoko going to do tonight?!" the girl asked.

"She is cleaning for the zoo keeper, whom you saw at the ticket office. She is washing his clothes, shining his shoes, making beds and filling the wash-basins."

"I thought she was the daughter of a king!"

The tutor gently kissed her golden hair.

"I have crown jewels," she felt, "like Lady Dudley, four rows of flawless pearls, inestimable in value, perhaps two million – – –."

The moist soil of the evening meadow offered its hazy, misty freshness to the tired people on those hard garden benches and to the lovers in secluded corners who longed for the evening and the silence. The stands of trees were grouped like clouds upon the meadow-firmament. Tíoko was shivering in the garden. She wrapped her thin, heliotrope-colored cotton shawl over her wonderful light brown breasts, which otherwise existed in freedom and beauty, as God had created them, offering the noble male gaze an image of earthly perfection, an ideal of strength and flowering.

Then she crouched on a little wooden stool and peeled potatoes for dinner.

"What is Tíoko doing?!" the child on the bench wondered.

The tutor held her white hand in his. These beautiful, brotherly hands – – –.

"Allons⁵ – – –," said the boy, "this is terribly boring and we are getting cold. Fortunatina is just about to catch a cold."

"Don't you worry about that, please, I ask you, please

---

⁵ French: Let's go.

– – –," said the tutor. Embarrassed, they all walked home in silence.

On the way home, the little girl said to the tutor, "But I might have caught a cold easily – – –. Are you angry with Oscar?!"

"Dear, gentle one – – –," said the tutor and pressed her little hand onto his heart.

THE CONVERSATION

"It is cold and quite damp here, Tíoko. Puddles everywhere. You people are practically naked. What are these flimsy linen things?! Your hands are cold, Tíoko. Let me warm them up for you. You need at least some cotton-flannel, not these thin threads."

"We are not permitted to wear anything, Sir, no shoes, nothing, we even have to take off the headscarf. 'Put it away,' says the zoo keeper, 'put it away. Or do you want to make like a lady?!'"

"Why doesn't he permit it?!"

"We are supposed to look like savages, Sir, like Africans. It is completely silly. In Africa we couldn't run around like this. We would be a laughing stock. Like bushmen, yes, just like them. Nobody lives in huts like these. In our country, huts are just for dogs, gbé. Quite foolish. They want us to look like animals. What do you think, Sir?! The zoo keeper says, 'Hey, there are plenty of Europeans here. Why would we need you?! You have to be naked, of course.' "

"You will get sick and die – –."

"Oh, Sir, at night we set up little tin containers in our huts filled with glowing embers. Oh, how warm that is. And Manomba's body is warm, I press up against her. And Akolé is warm, and little Dédé is really warm at night. Perhaps the sun will shine tomorrow. That will be nice for Tíoko."

"Tíoko – – – – –!"

"Sir – – –?!"

"Tíoko – – – – – – –."

"Sir, do you think that the sun will shine and be warm tomorrow?!"

"I hope so."

Fig. 4: School, Ashanti exhibit at the Vienna Zoological Garden. Gouache by Wilhelm Gause, 1897 (Wien Museum, Vienna).

THE SCHOOL

The little children have the gentlest eyes in the world. Eyes of paradise. If you hold these little black children close to your heart, they feel flattered. If you place your hand on their woolly heads, they look at you – – – – nobody could find the words for that!

"Just like our Bobo – – –," said a little girl. That didn't help anybody understand any better. "Are these black people really able to think?!" asked the little girl.

"My little dumbo – – –," the father replied proudly and glanced at his neighbor, who hadn't been listening and thus trampled on that proud fatherly expression, simply blew it away.

The names of the little boys are: Agô, Tájhviâ, Amŏn, Kódjŏ, Nôté, Swâté, Sábâh, Ofolukvakú. Pretty names, aren't they? Full of expression. They already know the following words in English:

song	=	lālā in their language.
monkey	=	adún
mouse	=	kwákwé
fly	=	adodón
cat	=	alonté
rat	=	obísji
knife	=	kâklá

Which language is more beautiful?!

Odji[6] is softer, at any rate. Here man himself truly has become sound, the entire human being is expressed in sound, it's not just some strange music. Like a dark gentle heart that would begin to speak –.

---

[6] The examples of Ghanaian language, which Altenberg – and Meyer's Encyclopedia of his days – call "Odschi" and "Odji" are, in fact, from one of the Dangme languages. I thank Samuel Mate-kodjo from Central College in Pella, Iowa, for his input on the question of languages spoken in Ghana.

These children cry without a sound. It is like an inner drama. The face remains untroubled. No complaint at all. The tears run down as though they weren't coming from the countenance, but were passing over it only by chance on their arduous journey.

The face is completely untroubled, while the tears are running – – –.

MULTIPLICATION TABLES

I am studying diligently:

èkó	1
enyo	2
eté	3
eduë	4
enumo	5
ekba	6
kbao	7
kbānyo	8
néhu	9
nyònma	10
...	

When bibi Akolé is tested, I prompt. Nobody notices. Only Jaté is smiling at me. The punishment is being struck on the head with a bamboo stick.

The teacher is quizzing bibi Akolé. 7? kbao. 4? eduë. 50? Nomajnumó. 21? – – –. 21? – – –. Bibi Akolé looks at me anxiously.

I don't answer. I have forgotten it too. Bibi Akolé looks at me anxiously.

I run into one of the huts, whip out my notebook, scribble 21 in it, and, with a questioning look, hold it up to the Negro woman. "Twenty one – –," she says, "what's the matter?!" "You educated cow," I think. "No, no," I say, "Ashantee?!" "Nomanjokāākomè," she says.

I'm flying back to school and in my excitement I shout out a little too loud, "Nomanjokāākomè!!".

All the children laugh. The teacher smiles kindly.

Bibi Akolé is crying in a corner.

A moment earlier, she had received her blow on the head.

I will probably forget the Ashantee multiplication tables – – –, but I will forever remember: 21 – – nomanjokāākomè!

Fig. 5: Ashanti men, Ashanti exhibit at the Vienna Zoological Garden. Gouache by Wilhelm Gause, 1897 (Wien Museum, Vienna).

THE HUTS (In the Evening)

The Chief's hut: From three hooks on the wall hang three pocket watches, a gold one, a silver one, and one made of nickel. The Chief sits on a plank-bed, playing minor chords on a harmonica. In a little open suitcase are white flannel pants. Madame Jaboley Domëi smokes a small pipe and listens to her husband play.

The hut of Nôthëi, the goldsmith: Agô (nine months), Taywiãh (four years), Akuōkó, and bibi Akolé are sleeping here. The hut of the goldsmith Nôthëi – – – palace of beauty, paradise of peace. Four breaths like accords of a redeemed world.

The young women's hut: big Akolé, Djôjô, Monámbō, Aschon, Tíōkŏ, Akóschia. There they squat in the evenings like frogs around a little candle that is placed on the floor; they eat, relax, smoke a fine cigarette, sing quietly and gently, apply camphor ointment, look at themselves in a little broken mirror, make delicate dance movements with the upper body, which is bare, and laugh with their free, untroubled souls, arrange their bead strands on hooks on the wall, envy Tíoko for her 7 strands (2 light green ones and one rose-colored one shaped like a rhombus, 2 garnet strands, 1 amber strand, 1 pearl necklace, a French imitation); they rave about light green and garnet, lie down on the hard floor, put out the candle stump, sing a little more and fall asleep.

That is the young women's hut.

The hut of the "young gentlemen": It is empty. The young gentlemen have gone into town for the evening. When will they return?! What will they experience?! Nobody knows. The young gentlemen's hut is empty.

44

Fig. 6: Dance performance, Ashanti exhibit at the Vienna Zoological Garden. Gouache by Wilhelm Gause, 1897 (Wien Museum, Vienna).

DINNER

How do the Ashanti dine?!

They squat on the floor. In a pot are snow-white mashed potatoes made with water and without salt and cold; in another pot some meat bouillon with peppers, actually a thin gulyas[7] broth. With their completely clean hands they scoop out a lump of mash, dip it into the meat bouillon and lick the mash off their fingers.

Akóschia: Slavic facial type. Madonna of Hynais[8], Bohemian-French. Necklace made of a thousand tiny light and dark brown beads. Earrings made of gold filigree. Flawless physique. Skin like silk.

Souper, donné aux Achanti par la Direction du "Tiergarten."[9]

I sit in between Akóschia and Djôdjô.

Menu: Boeuf braisé en Paprica,[10]
          Potatoes en sel,[11]
          Bière.[12]

Nothing out of the ordinary is happening. I cut the meat for Djôdjô. She gives me her best pieces. I give her my best. It's like the table-d'hôte[13] of the future!

Akóschia smiles – – –.

Her toga slides down.

There she sits in her grandeur!

I say, "Akóschia – – –."

"Yes, Sir – – –?!"

She senses: "He cannot say anything but my name.

---

[7] Gulyas or gulyás: A Hungarian dish.

[8] Vojtěch Hynais (1854-1925), artist in Prague.

[9] French: Dinner for the Ashanti provided by the management of the Zoological Garden.

[10] French: Braised beef with peppers.

[11] French: Salted potatoes.

[12] French: Beer.

[13] French: Dinner table.

How funny."

To this name I sing songs. Like Paganini[14] played on the G-string. One can manage with just one word – – – Akóschia!

"Do the ladies and gentlemen wish to have some more roast?!" the waiter asks with a smile and thinks himself a European, a person of higher standing.

I offer a cigarette to Akóschia, a Kyriazi Imperatore with a gold cigarette holder.

She smokes, leaning back a little.

My hand holds her hand; our fingers unite, celebrate their wedding.

"Akóschia – – –."

She smokes, smiling kindly, does not at all want to get up to take part in the Dance of the Fetish Priest, which is to be performed at ten o'clock, for the highly esteemed audience. "The priest," the posters read, "sets the fetish-priestess into a state of ecstasy, in which she – seemingly unconscious – is subject to his will – – – – – ."

I hold Akóschia's wonderful hand in mine.

Posters are not required. Akóschia leans back a little, smoking a Kyriazi Imperatore, smiles gently. Her skin glistens like silk.

"Akóschia – – –."

"Yes, Sir – – –."

The zoo keeper approaches, "Mademoiselle Akochie, do you wish to stay here or will you trouble yourself to participate in the Priest Dance?! Excuse us, Sir – – –."

Akóschia rises, shrouds her blossoming body in her toga, hiding it away as in a coffin, and walks away – – –.

"The Fetish Priest," the posters read," sets the Priestess into a state of ecstasy, in which – – –. The 'French Colony' appropriately calls it: 'faire la fétiche.'"[15]

Music can already be heard. Like the sound beneath a

---

[14] Nicolò Paganini (1782-1840), Italian violinist, violist, guitarist and composer.
[15] French: Performing the fetish.

rolling railway carriage crossing a bridge.

The Priestess is already in a state of ecstasy making dramatic movements.

Akóschia – – –! How calmly you sit – – –!

Faire la fétiche!

Fig. 7a and b: Children, Ashanti exhibit at the Vienna
Zoological Garden. Gouaches by Wilhelm Gause, 1897
(Wien Museum, Vienna).

THE KISS

I was sitting on a park bench in the Zoological Garden. On my lap sat bibi Akolé counting her money which was distributed beautifully into three purses, 25 Kreuzer in each compartment, presents from her admirers.

A very beautiful young lady came by with her husband.

Akolé looked at the lady, got up, walked over to her, opened her arms, and wanted to kiss her on the mouth because she was so beautiful.

The lady recoiled.

Deeply embarrassed, the child pressed herself close to me.

"Madame – –," I said, "I implore you, I implore you – – –."

"Not on the mouth – –," she said uneasily.

I embraced Akolé, kissed her beloved mouth, the breath of which was like a breeze from evening meadows.

"Why don't you do it – – –," her husband said, "il sera offensé.[16]"

"I can't – – –," said the very beautiful young lady.

So I said, "This lady is repelled by you, Akolé. I am behaving like a silly, stupid mother who doesn't understand others. Forgive me, Madame. I was acting like a stupid mother, the silliest and most narrow-minded thing on earth. The love of a bird's brain, as simple as that."

The lady gave the child a crown.

The child gave it right back.

The husband thought, "Was all that necessary?! Such hysterics."

The lady said good-bye, shook my hand, and looked at me sadly.

Slowly, the couple walked away.

---

[16] French: He will be offended.

Akolé tucked herself away in my arms, which held her with immeasurable love.

CULTURE

Akolé, the big Akolé (age 17), and Akolé, the bibi Akolé (age 7), were invited for dinner at Mrs. H.'s in the city. They wore brown togas and light green glass bead necklaces. Nothing else. Some friends of the family were present. The two Akolés ate like English ladies from the Queen's Court.

"A lot of imagination, these paradise people – – –," said Miss D.

"Yes, indeed!" Peter A. replied.

Miss D. blushed.

Peter A.: "A forest. What is a forest?! A lot of imagination, a forest. An accumulation of leaves. Let's not have any overly poetic notions, my dear friends, no unhealthy musing! That's what it is. An accumulation of leaves."

"Why do you always want to wound, Peter, to bring out the pillory, to guillotine?!"

Peter: "Negroes are children. Who understands them?! Negroes are just like sweet, silent nature. They strike a chord in you, while they themselves are without music. Ask what the forest is, the child, the Negro?! They are something that strikes a chord in us, the conductors of our symphony orchestra. They themselves don't play an instrument, they conduct our soul."

After dinner each of the Akolés received a wonderful French doll, for fun.

First they sang them to sleep and kissed them.

All of a sudden big Akolé let the toga slide down from her perfect shoulders and nursed the doll from her magnificent breast. Little Akolé stood there with her hungry little doll in her arms, in despair.

Mrs. H. told her guests that this was the most sacred moment of her life.

The guests concurred, even if their words were not so

pompous.

Even Monsieur R. de B. smiled in a way one doesn't really smile when one is smiling – – –.

PARADISE

"What would you like most in the world, Tíoko?!"
"Green bills cutted, Sir – – –." (Cut green glass beads)
"And what else?!"
"And purple bills cutted, Sir – – –."
"And what else?!"
"And nothing, Sir – –."

THE EVENING

Eight o'clock in the evening. Rain, rain – – –.

It stops for a little while.

A sweet fragrance of wet pebbles fills the air. Or at least it seems that way.

Tíoko is standing there, wrapped in purple cotton. Like a freezing dark water bird. She stands as if on one foot, nestled in purple feathers.

That's when I kiss her for the first time.

She stands quietly – – –.

How happy I am – – –.

The rain has stopped for a little while.

The sweet fragrance of wet pebbles fills the air.

"Good night, Tíoko – – – – – – –. Tíoko – – –!? – – – – – Tíoko?!"

"Oh Sir – – –."

A LETTER FROM ACCRA

(West Coast, Gold Coast)

A letter from Africa. When was it posted?! On July 20th. When did it arrive?! On August 26th. The tears of the senders have already dried, while those of the receivers are still flowing. Monambô's brother, 14 years old, has passed away. "He was as tall as Tíoko – – –," says Monambô, "and just as beautiful."

Big Akolé sits at her sales table, counting her money. Tears run down her noble face.

"Il me semble, qu'elle est encore plus noire aujourd'hui,[17]" says the daughter of a French secretary and kisses her.

"Was he related to her?!" I ask the Chief in English.

"We cry about everyone," says the Chief, "that is how 'Black-men' are. When I am back in Africa, I will cry about you, Sir."

Akóschia sits on the dance floor in the arena, playing music with iron castanets; tears run down her noble countenance.

Tíoko sits outside her house, singing quietly to herself and crying. Like a harp accompanying tears. Like psalms.

Monambô is not crying.

"Are you not sad, Monambô?!"

"Sir, I am far from home. I will cry until I am back in Africa – – –."

"Isn't this communal mourning a little hard to understand?" says the daughter of the secretary to me, timidly.

"Don't think that it is this young man these noble, gentle creatures are grieving over. They cry about Africa,

---

[17] French: It seems to me that she is even blacker today.

c'est le mal du pays,[18] the most tender disease of our soul that is coming to light. Just like a little girl getting a new nanny. 'Strange,' say the concerned parents, 'really, none of us would have expected anything like it, our darling has been so friendly with her; just like old friends. Everything is going fine, they get along fine, and the nanny is really so very sweet with her, she doesn't have an easy situation.' Suddenly an insignificant word from the nanny, a gesture. And the child bursts out into tears. Is it the word, the gesture?! Not at all. She is sobbing for her old nanny – – –."

Nine o'clock in the evening. The tears have dried. The moon makes the birch in the garden glisten. The African huts are silent. Tíoko's hut is dark. Monambô calls me. I enter the hut. Lying on the floor are Monambô, Akolé the wonderful, and Akóschia. No matting, no blanket. Their perfect upper bodies are naked. A fragrance of noble, clean, young bodies. Quietly, I touch the wonderful Akolé.

"Go to Tíoko," she says gently, "you love her."

Monambô who wants to save her sadness for Africa says, "Sir, tomorrow you must bring us a chamber pot; it is too cold to step outside the hut, at night. It must be blue on the outside and white on the inside. The three of us together will pay whatever it costs. If it were for Tíoko, you would surely give it to her as a present! How much will it be?!"

"Monambô, I never bought a chamber pot in my life. I know nothing about the prices. Between 50 Kreuzer and 500 Gulden. Queens use gold ones."

"Sir, today has been a sad day. Good night. You love Tíoko. The chamber pot must be blue on the outside and white on the inside. Make sure to bring it tomorrow. We can't step outside the hut during these nights, you understand?!"

I kissed the hands of these three girls on their hard resting-places. Akolé was simply too beautiful! I kneeled

---

[18] French: It is homesickness.

down, kissed her forehead, her eyes, her mouth – –.

"Go to Tíoko – – –," she said gently.

Monambô and Akóschia huddled up in their cotton blankets.

When I stepped out of the hut, the birches were gray in first light of dawn, as if they were at one with the misty air which smelled of moist freshness – – –.

THE NEGRO

A wonderful little blond girl who is blind in one eye is dragging a giant Negro around with her, everywhere. In the circus, they sit in a private box by themselves.

"A little romantic – – –," her father says happily and proudly, "if it goes on like this – – –?!"

Terrifying pictures in American tabloids: "A Negro rapes a little girl. The mob lynches him, pours gasoline over him, and he smolders for two hours."

There they sit together in the private box, in the circus. Something magnetic, some universal sympathy, the condensors of accumulated love that flows from nature: the soul of the child and the spinal marrow of the savage!

The American tabloids exaggerate. But nature herself is an exaggeration: the thunderstorm, the thunderbolt, Vesuvius, love, the rain forest, the herrings' migration, everything is an exaggeration – – – – – –!

"This is an elephant – – – ," says the little girl, "elephant."

"Shuo – – ," says the Negro.

"Shuo– –," says the child.

How close they have become: shuo–elephant, elephant–shuo. They already speak a common language: shuo–elephant, elephant–shuo!

Fig. 8: Ashanti village, Ashanti exhibit at the Vienna Zoological Garden. Gouache by Wilhelm Gause, 1897 (Wien Museum, Vienna).

AKOLÉ

"This one is supposedly the most beautiful," the visitors say, "a beauté[19] in her homeland. Where is this Ashanti anyway?! Well, for a Negro woman – – –. She's a proud one, quite unappealing. Who does she think she is, this little moor?! Are we supposed to consider it an honor to buy her junk?! She doesn't even want to look at us while she takes our money for Le Ta Kotsa, a dental twig. It's surely all a swindle. Are you homesick?! Our saleswomen would do a bad business that way. You have to be friendly, darling, nobody is doing you any harm. She is freezing, poor creature. No, no, no, no, don't be so quick to bristle! What's your station back home?! Some kind of a lady?! In the end, you will sell it for less. Arrogant little brat. Adieu.[20] Can't get anything out of her. Good-bye, little moor, don't hurt yourself. Things will surely get better. Bye."

"Bènjo, bènjo------------!" (Go to hell, get lost.)

---

[19] French: Beauty.
[20] French: Bye.

AKOLÉ'S SINGING, AKOLÉ'S SWEET SONG

A terrible storm in the garden. Thousands of green leaves and little black branches cover the brown pond. The light brown wild geese get ruffled feathers and open their red bills.

Akolé is sitting by the pond, singing her sweet song:
"andelaína andelaína andelaína gbomolééééé – –
andelaína gbomolé.
andelaína Akkraūma, andelaína gbomolé
andelaína andelaína – – –.
andelaína hé oblāinŏ, andelaína gbomolé – – –
andelaína andelaína andelaína gbomolé.
andelaína A k k r a-lédé andelaína, hé oblāinŏ
andelaína andelaína – – –.
andelaína V i e n n a-lédé andelaína bobandôôô –
andelaína andelaína andelaína bobandôôô."

A terrible storm in the garden. Thousands of green leaves and little black branches cover the brown pond.
"andelaína andelaína – – – – – –."

COMPLICATIONS

Akolé, like a bust by Barbédienne[21] cast in bronze, a young man of means would like to possess you!

In your frizzy hair you wear a little gold comb he gave you!

He drives up in a horse-drawn carriage. His mother wears a hat made from French violets, Akolé, and greets you with a smile: "It would be an ideal moment in Victor's life, something that would save him from ... She doesn't speak any language. We have her under control. She belongs to us. She is devoted to me. What more could she want?! Another glass bead necklace and then one more. And a silk umbrella and sandals. She is black, not everybody's taste, dumb to everyone. No complications de l'âme.[22] She might be an ideal moment in his life, just what the doctor ordered for his apathetic, exhausted soul, a veritable tonic. At any rate, something out of the ordinary, like a trip abroad, or a year of military service. Something transformative, activating. Something like an episode in an artist's or poet's life. Later, of course, – –?!"

"Akolé – – –," says Ofolu Ahadjí, "misumo (I love you) – – –."

"Akolé – – –," says Peter A., "go back to Accra – –!"

"Akolé – – –!" says the young man of means, who would like to possess her.

The mother doesn't say anything at all; tenderly, she kisses the girl's forehead – – –.

---

[21] Ferdinand Barbédienne (1810-1892), caster of bronze sculptures and founder of the bronze foundry of Barbédienne, Paris.

[22] French: Complications of the soul.

PHYSIOLOGICAL FEATURES

Can Negro women blush?!

Negro women can blush. They turn copper-colored, lighter so to speak. For example, when you kiss their hands and behave like a gentleman.

Can Negro women turn pale?!

No, on the contrary. They – – – turn dark!

For example, when you – – – don't behave like a gentleman.

Then – – – they turn dark!

LITTLE ELLA

"Ella, please behave properly. Old Mary is going to pick you up at seven o'clock in the evening. Can we expect Mr. Peter to bring you back from the Zoological Garden so late at night?! It is enough for him to pick you up. Why does he do that, anyway?! Well. Just be sensible. I believe you will have enough time to have fun."

"To have fun, Mama?!"

"That's right. Well, it isn't exactly a piano lesson, to go to the Zoological Garden to those savages with Mr. Peter. Let's not overdo it, you understand me?! You know that I am happy to allow everything that – – –. Ella – – ! Ella – – ?! What is the matter? You are already quite hysterical. No, you are too foolish. My angel. No, no, no – – –. Now look, was that necessary? In a minute I will forbid it, altogether – – –. Here, take my handkerchief. You silly fool. How old are you, tell me?! Eh?! Go on, my darling, don't be silly."

"Oh, Mama – – –. It is not for fun. He introduces me to another life in this Zoological Garden. Everything is so wonderful. Nobody can say why!? 'We're like trout in a stream down there,' said Mr. Peter once about us, about himself and about me, Mama."

"It's all right, my child. But if Papa knew all that?! At night, you'll be tossing and turning again. And you'll look bad in the morning."

"Oh, Mama. Mr. Peter told me on the way: 'I can be myself around you. One doesn't have to lie about anything.' Do you understand that, Mama?!"

"Well, what does it mean?!"

"I don't know what it means. I feel it!"

"See, those are unhealthy things. But, I promised you and I will keep my word. Go and wash your face, he will be here any second."

"Mama, I want to stay home –."

"Why?!"

"I would so like to stay home!"

"Well, see, you are already all confused. Just as he is. Go, my child, go, get dressed, wash your face and take that light green velvet hat. Hurry, get ready. Don't make me cross. I already told old Mary to pick you up at the Zoological Garden at seven o'clock. What is the matter with you?! One minute this way, the next minute that way?!"

"Mama, I want to stay home –."

"Ella, don't make me angry."

— —

Mr. Peter rings the bell down the hall next to the house telephone.

Through the speaking tube, "Send Ella down, right away."

"Doctor, Ella isn't feeling too well. Unfortunately she will not be able to go to the Zoological Garden with you. Thank you so very much for your kindness."

"Oh – –. May I speak to Ella?! – – – – –. Ella, don't you want to come into the fairy kingdom?!"

"No, Doctor, I cannot go into the fairy kingdom."

"Adieu."

"Adieu, Doctor, oh, Doctor –."

Nothing else is heard.

Fig. 9: Ashanti procession, Ashanti exhibit at the Vienna Zoological Garden. Gouache by Wilhelm Gause, 1897 (Wien Museum, Vienna).

A LETTER FROM VIENNA
(To the Negro Woman Monambô)[23]

My dear Monambô!

*As I only know one single word in Odschi, "misoumo" (I love
you), which may be enough for the simple happieness in life, but too
little for the sad days, so I cannot talk with Nabadû and you must
be so kind, dear Monambô, to read to her my stupid letter, which is a
bit of my stupid heart. Dear Monambô, the first day when Nabadû
came from the Ashantee-village in Buda-Pesth to Vienna, I was in
the Arena. Nabadû came in. Nabadû sat down quite near me. She
leaned her head on my shoulder, put her hand on my knee. So we
stopped sitting and I was like in a drunkenness of happiness. Never
before had I seen her. And she leaned her head on my shoulder! The
same evening she sat before her hut and sung sad things of Africa.
When I went up to her, she didn't keep silence like all the others,
like birds in a wood. But she sung and sung, as if no stranger would
have been near her. And so it was! That was the last day of my
happiness, dear Monambô. Beginning from this day she was quite
altered. Like a stranger she got towards me. I always remember this
magic first day, when Nabadû arrived from Buda-Pesth, quite a
stranger to me and leaned her head on my shoulder!*

Oh dear Monambô, do not laugh – –.

*Like a sickness remains this evening in me, when Nabadû
behaved as if I had been a brother or a home, like Akkra or the
whole of Africa. Why did she put her head on my shoulder?! It
makes a heart sick, when it is for one evening full of happiness and
for all the others full of sorrow.*

*I suppose, the reason of all this will be the joung 'Black-man'
Noë Salomon Dowoonnah.*

*Say to Nabadû that, when she returns to Akkrâ, a white man
will for ever remain sick after this one evening, when Nabadû leaned*

---

[23] In the original German-language text, this letter is written in
English and followed by a German translation. For purposes
of authenticity, the original (faulty) English has not been
corrected in this edition. In the original, this letter is not
italicized.

her head on his shoulder like on the shoulder of a friend – – – – –!!
Dear Monambô, do not laugh – – –.

Jours

Peter.

friends among the Ashanti women at the Vienna Ashanti
exhibit, 1896.
"Mísŭmô sanì! Peter Altenberg" (I love you! Peter
Altenberg).
"Òzà Afrika, kai mi tshüi ewoahè, kai mi tshüi ègbò!! PA"
"Nāh-Badûh from Accra, Gold Coast, West Africa."
(Peter Altenberg's photo collection, Wien Museum,
Vienna)

TRANSLATION OF "A LETTER FROM VIENNA"[24]

My dear Monambô!

Since I only know one single word in "Odschi," misoumo (I love you), which may be enough to express simple happiness in life, but not enough to express its sad days, I cannot communicate with Nah-Badûh, and you must be so kind as to read my silly letter to her, which expresses a part of my silly heart.

Dearest Monambô, the first day when Nah-Badûh came from the Ashanti village in Budapest to Vienna, I was in the arena. Nah-Badûh came in. Nah-Badûh sat down next to me. Very close to me. She rested her head on my shoulder and placed her hand on my knee. We quietly sat like this and I felt drunk with happiness. I had never seen her before, nor had she ever seen me. And she rested her head on my shoulder!

The very same evening, she sat outside her house, singing sad things from Africa.

When I walked up to her she didn't fall silent like all the others, like birds in the woods. But she kept on singing, as if no stranger had approached. And so it was.

That was the last day of my happiness, dear Monambô.

Since that day she has changed. She treats me like a stranger. I always remember this magic first day, when Nah-Badûh arrived from Budapest, quite a stranger to me, and rested her head on my shoulder!

Oh dear Monambô, do not laugh – – –.

That evening when Nah-Badûh treated me as if I were her brother or a home, like Accra or the whole of Africa, remains with me like a sickness.

---

[24] In the original German-language text, this segment suggests the translation of Peter's letter from English into German.

I suppose the reason for all this is the young Ashanti man Noë Salomon Dovoonnâh.

Dear Monombô, please tell Nahbadûh that, if she returns to Accra, a white man will remain sick forever as a result of this one evening, when Nahbadûh rested her head on his shoulder as if it were the shoulder of a friend –!!

Dear Monambô, do not laugh – – –.

Yours,

Peter.

THE PRINCESS IN GREEN

Presents for Nahbadû from Sir Peter:

4 strings of pale green beads.

5 strings of emerald imitations (Paris).

8 strings of dark green opaque beads for a garter-belt, with a dark green, little silk scarf which one fastens on the bead belt and pulls between the legs.

8 green glass hairpins (Venetian).

White shoes lined with green silk.

A white flannel bodice lined with green silk.

4 duku (headscarf) made of green silk.

A pagne[25] (cloak, toga), 4 meters long, made of green silk.

---

[25] French: A piece of clothing typical of Africa. The term refers to loin-cloths as well as togas. Altenberg uses "pagne" to refer to both women's and men's togas.

Fig. 11: Kitchen, Ashanti exhibit at the Vienna Zoological Garden. Gouache by Wilhelm Gause, 1897 (Wien Museum, Vienna).

HOT PEPPERS

"Sir – – –," said Nôthëi, the goldsmith, "where are the hot peppers you promised to bring?!"

"I forgot, Nôthëi – – –."

"You forgot?! You probably did not feel like buying them!? Nahbadû didn't eat anything for lunch today – –."

"Why?!"

"Well – – –. By the way, there were no peppers in the soup. Black men don't eat anything without spices. That's why she did not touch it. Oh Sir, tomorrow you will not say, 'I forgot' –!"

L'HOMME MÉDIOCRE [26]

"Please tell me, what's the story with these young black girls?! – – – Won't you?!"

"No."

"Oh, you are a gentleman; you will not tell a thing."

"I have nothing to tell."

"Well, so, do they accept money?!"

"Yes."

"And silk scarfs?!"

"Yes."

"And then, what?"

"Then, nothing."

"Why do people give them presents?!"

"Because they are beautiful and gentle. They give us royal presents and we thank them like beggars."

"And what about the young men?! They have been away from home for eight months. What do they do about – – –?!"

"They work, dance, sing –."

"But aren't they quite strong?!"

"That is exactly why. Only the weak have inescapable urges. The strong have powers of adaptation!"

"So the girls are unapproachable?!"

"On the contrary."

"Under which conditions?!"

"Under the condition of love."

"But I was told you could buy young black girls?!"

"That's right. If she loves you. You tell her mother, 'Māmă, I love your daughter and your daughter loves me.' 'So, you will have to give me 300 Schillings in silver,' replies the mother."

"How long can you keep the girl?!"

"As long as the love lasts, half a year, a year, two years,

---

[26] French: The average man.

forever."

"And if you dismiss her?!"

"Then she will be like a virgin. Any black man will marry her. How has she changed?! *Out of love* there is only *Immaculate Conception!*"

Pause.

"Nah-Badûh– –! Nah-Badûh, bāä (come here)! This gentleman asked me to give you these 10 Kronen for him."

"Oh, Sir – – –!?"

Fig. 12: Ashanti village, Ashanti exhibit at the Vienna Zoological Garden. Gouache by Wilhelm Gause, 1897 (Wien Museum, Vienna).

THE MACHINE

"Sir – – –," said the young Negro Mensah, "there is a magic thing (a mystery) in this garden. You put in two Káple (Kreuzer) and you learn your future."

"That's right," said Peter A.

"Sir, it is a really strange story: There is a Negro woman in the upper village, and I love her. But she has a husband."

"Does she love him?!"

"No."

"How do you know?!"

"Her eyes are too sad."

"Come – – –."

The gentleman and the Negro walked up to the fortune-telling machine. It was varnished bright red and had a panel with a pointer. Wherever the pointer stopped lay your destiny.

The Negro put in two Káple.

The pointer turned.

It stopped on the words: "You will undertake a journey and earn a lot of money unexpectedly."

"Well – –?!" said the Negro.

"You are loved," said Peter A.

"Sir," said the Negro to Peter A., the next day, "fancy that?! There is another one of these magic things in the garden. If this one says the same thing – – –!?"

"First show me Méja, your beloved girl-friend."

He took the gentleman there.

Méja sat on the dance floor in the arena. Her husband walked up to her, took off his pagne made from gray-green wool, and wrapped it around her delicate shoulders, because the evening wind began to rise in the garden.

She remained motionless.

"Come – – –," said the gentleman to the Negro.

The blue varnished machine worked precisely.

The pointer stopped.

"Well – –?!" said Mensah.

"A great misfortune lies ahead. But there is still time. Think it over!" said the gentleman, while the machine indicated happiness and love.

Mensah became rapt in deep thought –.

"Thank you, Sir."

Pause.

Then, Mensah said, "And yet, her eyes are too sad –."

But the gentleman thought, "He wrapped his toga around her when the evening wind began to rise – – –!"

ADULTERY

"And what are the consequences of adultery in your culture, Samson Adukuè?!?"

"What do you mean, Sir?!?"

"Well, does the husband beat his wife, does he send her back to her parents, does he go as far as to kill her?!?"

"Why should he do that, Sir?!? After all, he married her because he loves her!?"

"Well, there must be some consequences to adultery?!?"

"Oh yes, Sir, terrible consequences. Up to then, she has been his great love, from then on she is merely his little love!"

BEATINGS

"Beatings are good, oh Sir," the young Negro woman
Dédé, who had just been beaten by her husband, said to P.
A., "It is like tshofán (medicine)! The person who is doing
the beating is healed of his anger and the other of his 'bad
conscience'!"

THE DOWRY

"How do you people handle the question of dowry, Samson Adukuè!!?"

" The man who wants to marry a girl, oh Sir, pays a sum to her parents, naturally, in order to get the girl!"

"Naturally!!"

HEREDITARY SUCCESSION

"How do you people determine the sole heir?!!"

"The oldest son of the *sister* of the deceased, of course!"

"What do you mean?!? The nephew? Well, why not the person's own son?!?"

"The person's own son?! Why would he be the heir?! The son of the *sister* is, after all, the only sure blood relation! The son of my sister, whoever his father may be – a husband or an adulterer – must have my blood, he is my sister's son! My own son?!? Oh, Sir!?"

PHILOSOPHY

Visitors to the Ashantee-village knock on the wooden walls of the huts, just for the fun of it.

Nôthëi, the goldsmith: "Sir, if you came to our place in Accra as exhibits, we would not knock on your huts in the evening!"

CHIVALRY

"Sir – – –," said Chief Bôdjé to P. A., "come into my hut."

— — — — — —.

"Sit down."

— — — — — —.

"This afternoon, I beat Nahbadû. I beat her with this bullwhip. Do you understand me?!"

"I understand – – –."

"I am the chief of my people. I don't like beating Nahbadû. Of course. However, whenever all the girls go to the tam-tam (dancing and singing), she stays behind in her hut doing nothing. She is neither sick nor tired. She sits in her hut totally crazy, doing nothing. I am the chief of my people! I asked her why she was doing the same thing, every day, sitting there and doing nothing. I asked and asked. Then I beat her with my bullwhip. What if all the girls sat in the huts day-dreaming, eh?! What do the white people pay for?! It is our duty. I don't like beating Nahbadû. I just wanted to tell you that, so you know. Anything wrong with you, Sir – –?!"

"Nothing, Bôdjé – – –."

"Well, Sir, from now on I will leave her to daydream in her hut – – –."

MOTHERHOOD

"Oh, Sir," said a young, completely careworn Negro woman to P. A., "take from my little Akolé, Akòshia, Mensah, Shômé the sweet beauty that I have given them, put it all back together, and you could admire me just as much as your divine Nāh-Badûh who has not yet given away a thing!"

Fig. 13: Peter Altenberg and an Ashanti woman in a
Vienna coffee house. Lithograph by Bertha Czegka, 1902,
printed in: *Schwarz auf Weiß. Wiener Autoren den Wiener
Kunstgewerbeschülern zu ihrem Feste am 6. Februar 1902.* Wien:
Verlag des Comités für das Fest der Kunstgewerbeschüler,
1902 (Dokumentationsstelle, Literaturhaus, Vienna).

LE COEUR [27]

A cold September evening. If only I had knitted English gloves! How nice an over-coat lined with polecat fur would be. Such dreams, my dear?! What are you complaining about?! These beautiful brown girls have only a pagne to wear. That is as if one of our sixteen-year-olds, a fragile human springtime, were sitting in a red and blue swim suit in the Prater[28] in the fall!

Yet, the newspapers write, "Our black foreigners in the Zoological Garden have not suffered any loss of their good spirits. The business venture continues to make every effort for the viewing public – – –."

The wind sends a chill through the ash-trees – – –. Brrr, the people are shivering.

Djôjô comes out of the younger girls' hut and says to Peter A., "Come!" Inside the hut, Tíoko sits on the floor, surrounded by her girl-friends Djôjô, Ashüë, Kôkô, Lomlé, Ashôn. A little candle is burning on the floor.

Tíoko takes a black ribbon and ties Peter A.'s hands together, tightly. She extinguishes the candle.

Silence. Darkness.

Tíoko: "Nabadû all (N. is everything) – – – Tíoko finish (It's over with Tíoko). Tíoko no fine, Tíoko no good, Tíoko no beautiful, Tíoko ugh, ugh, ugh. Nabadû good, Nabadû fine, Nabadû beautiful. Nabadû ashinô (glass beads), Nabadû duku (headscarf), Nabadû all (Nabadû gets everything). Nabadû cold, Nabadû brrr, Nabadû shoes! Tíoko cold, Tíoko brrr, Tíoko no shoes! Fléflé (wretch)!"

Ashôn, Ashüë, Lomlé, Djôjô: "No fléflé! Sir Peter good, Tíoko good, Nabadû good – – –."

Tíoko: "Tíoko finish (It's over with Tíoko) – – –."

She lights the little candle again and unties the black

---

[27] French: The heart.

[28] Vienna's amusement park since 1766.

ribbon from Mr. Peter's hands.

Silence – – –.

Tíoko: "Nabadû – – – Noé Salomon Dovoonnah!!!"

Peter A., mildly: "I know. Never mind (what's the difference)?!"

Silence.

Tíoko gently: "Nabadû no Salomon. Poor Salomon Africa, poor Tíoko Africa. Nabadû no Africa – – –. Nabadû Sir Peter!"

The girl-friends: "Nabadû Vienna – ! Nabadû Sir Peter!"

Mr. Peter takes Tíoko's freezing hand. She gently lifts it to his mouth for him to kiss: "Nabadû Vienna (N. will stay in Vienna with you), Nabadû no Salomon – – – –. Tíoko no good – –."

The girl-friends: "Tíoko good, Sir Peter good, Salomon good, Nabadû good. Nabadû Vienna, Vienna, Vienna – – –!"

Tíoko quietly leaves the hut – –.

Outside, the wind sends a chill through the ash-trees – – –.

"Tíoko, bää (come here) – – –!"

No answer – – – – –.

CONCLUSION

Mr. Peter sits in the arena of the Zoological Garden. Nabadû comes in, sits down next to him. She rests her head on his shoulder and places her wonderful hand on his knee. Just as before.

He is as if in a state of drunken happiness.

In the evening, she sits outside her hut, singing sad things from Africa. He walks up to her. She doesn't fall silent like all the others, like birds in the woods. As if no stranger had approached!

And so it was.

– – – – – –

Late that evening, the young Negro Noë Salomon Dovoonnah calls on Mr. Peter. "Sir, may I have a word! – –."

"What is the matter – –?! We have no business with one another – –!"

"You could give me an old overcoat of yours, Sir, it is really too cold in Europe –."

Mr. Peter takes off his overcoat with the English black and white lining, saying, "Take this one."

"Oh, it is brand new – – –."

"Take it."

"Sir, you will be cold on your way home."

"No, I will not be cold on my way home. I am warm. This night is like spring, all warm and mild – – –."

"Oh – – –!?"

THE COUNCIL (ASSEMBLY OF THE MEN)

Evening. The stars are sparkling. The village lies there, peacefully.

Outside the goldsmith's hut, Nôthéi, Adû, Kwakû, and Bôdjé sit on bamboo stools.

They are sitting, totally absorbed, in male contemplation.

Bôdjé: "You ought to know, Nôthéi! I suppose we will give Tíoko to the white man who has been our kind master here, the managing director of this garden. Can we do anything else? I suppose, this is what we'll do."

Deep silence.

Adû: "Bôdjé! I agree, this is what we'll do."

Deep silence.

Bôdjé: "Call Tíoko!"

"Tíoko, bää – – –!"

Bôdjé: "Tíoko, the council has decided to give you as a farewell present to the master of this garden. He has always been kind to us. We are black men, of course. Do you want to stay behind with him?!"

"I want to stay behind in Vienna – –."

"With the kind master of this garden?!"

Deep silence.

Tíoko: "With the master of this garden – – –. Does Mr. Peter know about this?!"

Bôdjé: "What concern is that of his?! The council has made its decision. Go!"

– –

The director of the Zoological Garden: "Gentlemen and Ladies! You will be amazed. This morning, the 'Council of the Men' gave me Tíoko as a gift of honor!"

"Hohohoho – – . And will you keep her?! Yes, you must. It will be a romantic story. Like a chapter by Victor

Hugo or Dumas[29] in our barracks!"

The director was silent.

Then he said, "It would not be a romantic story. The world is empty. Here with us, she would soon become an ostracized maid. Nevertheless, I have learned to love these black people. Against my own will. When I refused Tíoko, they all froze, deeply ashamed. They wanted to cry. I kissed Tíoko. Then Bôdjé said, 'Sir, since you don't want to accept Tíoko, because you don't like her, of course, allow me to give you this great bird rifle as a souvenir. I even shot a heron with it.'"

"How did Tíoko take it?!" the ladies asked.

"She stood there, straight as a ramrod, watching as she was replaced by a bird rifle. And do you know, Gentlemen and Ladies, what Mr. Peter said to me when he learned about this?!"

"Surely some terrible madness."

"That's right. He said, 'You should have kept her. You would have gotten along nicely with her.'"

"What did he mean?!"

"I don't know. But I also think that I would have gotten along nicely with her."

Everybody fell silent, as if ill at ease.

Then Miss Hansi H. said, "Director, could you please send Tíoko to our table?"

"What for?"

"I would like to kiss her on the forehead –."

---

[29] French novellists Victor-Marie Hugo (1802-1885) and Alexandre Dumas (1802-1870).

THE DAY OF DEPARTURE

Māmā of Tíoko: "Sir, come into our hut – – –."
– – – – – –.

"As a dash (present) we give you this little African wooden stool that our daughter Tíoko liked to sit on and cry. We give it to you in remembrance that you once loved our daughter – – –."

Nah-Badûh: "Poor?" (Are you poor?)
"Yes."
"No Africa?" (Can't you come to Africa with us?)
"No."
Silence.
"Dash-Goodbye?!" (What will you give me for a farewell present?!)
"Pagne, green silk and white" (toga made of green and white silk fabric).
"Good (That is good), yard eba (6 meters)."
"Yard eba."
"Yard banyô (8 meters)."
"Yard banyô. Noë Salomon Africa Nahbadûh??"
"And you could give me some money for the journey (shika, shika, good-bye)."
"I will give you 30 Schillings. Oh Nahbadûh – – –."
"Poor ... no Africa! Rich ... Africa!" (You cannot go to Africa with me, because you are poor. If you were rich, you would go with me!)
She stood there in her brown, naked beauty like a queen of life, "If you were rich, you would go with me, all the way to Africa!"

That is what sustains a queen! Victory!! The breath of victory!!

He would go with me all the way to Africa!

LE DÉPART POUR L'AFRIQUE [30]

Nah-Badûh (from the carriage window): "Mister Peter finishi, Mr. Peter finish (It is over with Mr. Peter). Mister Peter misumă (Mr. Peter loved me). Mister Peter Vienna (Mr. Peter is staying behind in Vienna). Mr. Peter finishi, Mr. Peter finish – – –!"

"Nah-Badûh – – –!"

"– – –?! – – –?!"

Slowly, she climbs from the carriage down to him on the platform –.

– – – – –

– – – – – – – –.

The bell! The bell!! The bell!!!

Slowly, Nah-Badûh climbs into the carriage –.

Finishi!

---

[30] French: Departure for Africa.

HER ADDRESS

Nah-Badûh
Christiansborg
Gold Coast, Accra
King's Street, Lômô-house
West Coast, Africa.

AN EVENING IN LATE FALL

"Director – – –," said the guard of the Zoological Garden, "there was a gentleman here tonight, asking for you. He then entered one of the huts in the upper village. A quarter of an hour later, he came back out and slowly left the garden."

"It's all right, Joseph. By the way, we'll tear down the huts, tomorrow – –. We need space for the tightrope-walkers and the ballon captif.[31]

---

[31] French: Tethered balloon.

Fig. 14: "Katidja - - - 1910, at the Abyssinian village. Nāh-Badûh - - - 1896, at the Ashanti village. In the meantime, I have become an old man - - -. But the enthusiasm remains; now as much as ever. - - -. Peter Altenberg"

(Peter Altenberg's photo collection, Wien Museum, Vienna).

Afterword
by
Katharina von Hammerstein

"Black is Beautiful," Viennese Style:

Peter Altenberg's *Ashantee* (1897)

The Vienna Café Central on Herrengasse is famous for its endless variety of coffees and cakes, but even more importantly, for its place in history as meeting place for the intelligentsia and bohème of Vienna around 1900. On your right as you enter, the life-sized figure of Peter Altenberg (1859-1919) sits at one of the marble-topped tables. Altenberg was one of the most eccentric members of the coffeehouse culture that formed around writers like Arthur Schnitzler (1862-1931) and Karl Kraus (1874-1936) in fin-de-siècle Vienna. It was the end of an era of Austrian imperial glory, yet a vibrant time in Austrian cultural production thanks to a progressive group of artists, writers, composers, and architects dedicated to shedding traditions and to exploring the stimulating multinational and multicultural character of the Habsburg Empire.

Peter Altenberg, whose real name was Richard Engländer, was born into a family of assimilated Jews in Vienna. His father was a wealthy business man, his mother a much admired, elegant lady of society. In his youth, Altenberg suffered from hypersensitivity of his nervous system, was a bad student, and later abandoned several attempts at professional training. As an adult, he enjoyed a bohemian lifestyle, falling in love either with women who were already claimed or with adolescent girls decades his junior. He was a hypochondriac and repeatedly sought treatment for his excessive consumption of drugs and alcohol. He lived in hotel rooms most his adult life and in order to pay his bills often had to rely upon Austro-German calls for donations on his behalf, some by renowned colleagues like Hermann Hesse (1877-1962), Hugo von Hofmannsthal (1874-1929), Gabriele Reuter (1859-1941), and Max Reinhardt (1873-1943). Despite this less than successful track record by bourgeois standards,

Altenberg was greatly admired by famous contemporaries (such as writers Franz Kafka 1883-1924, Rainer Maria Rilke 1875-1926, and Stefan Zweig 1881-1942, architect Adolf Loos 1870-1933, and painter Oskar Kokoschka 1886-1980) for the emotional immediacy of his impressionistic telegram style and his condensed prose, which focuses on the essential. Without any claim to social criticism per se, many of his works represent critical observations of contemporary Viennese society. Journalist Max Messer praised Altenberg in a 1897 review of *Ashantee* euphorically as "luminary and illuminator, a poet and prophet of future humanity."[1]

Today, we live in this prophesied future; in our global information age migration and electronic media have brought distant cultures closer. And in the context of current debates about the challenges of crosscultural, multicultural, and multiethnic coexistence, literary representations of white Europeans' historical encounters with cultural and "racial"[2] alterity – such as depicted in Altenberg's *Ashantee* (1897) – enjoy renewed interest. Shifting away from Eurocentric concepts that focus on one-directional cultural transmission from the "civilized," European metropolis to the "barbarian," non-European periphery, postcolonial approaches in the fields of historical, cultural, and literary studies have introduced a scholarly emphasis on intercultural exchange, dialog, and "contact zones," a term coined by Mary Louise Pratt for "social spaces where cultures meet, clash and grapple with each other, often in contexts of highly asymmetric relations of power."[3] In this context, the history of Blacks in Europe and its relationship to European colonialism in Africa has been rediscovered.

Admittedly, the Austro-Hungarian Empire had no overseas colonies,[4] yet, national tensions in the multi-national Habsburg Empire[5] and the ethnically diverse society of its vibrant capital Vienna around 1900 inspired a lively and often controversial discourse about the construction of individual, ethnic, and national identities through differentiation between Self and Other. Literature of turn-of-the-century Vienna served as a space that allowed for wishes, anxieties, and myths about Self and Other to be represented and, at times, questioned.

The fictionalized depictions of cross-cultural encounters between Austrians and Ashanti in Peter Altenberg's *Ashantee* of 1897 may serve as an example to illustrate an ambivalence characteristic of modern Western thought: the ambivalence between integrative acceptance of the cultural and ethnic Other as fellow human being on one hand and colonial discourse confirming white European hegemony on the other. I read Altenberg's *Ashantee* as an early literary representation of clearly well-intended and humane cross-cultural exchange between Europeans and Africans which is nonetheless peppered with examples of stereotypical cultural and racial differentiation and essentialization – in the sense of assigning certain attributes to certain ethnic groups – based on what we would call today Eurocentric, racist, and sexist perspectives.[6]

In *Ashantee*, a collection of thirty-eight impresssionist semi-autobiographical sketches, Altenberg, barely disguised as the work's autobiographical character called Sir Peter and Peter A., describes his protagonist's friendly relationship with a group of Ashanti tribes-people from the Gold Coast of Africa (the former British colony known today as Ghana). The literary text is dedicated to five Ashanti women who, along with one hundred-and-twenty countrymen and women, had been installed in 1896 as living objects in a popular ethnographic exhibit in the Vienna Tiergarten (Zoological Garden), then still located in Vienna's famous amusement park called Prater.[7]

Ideologically, the exhibit's location in the *Tier*garten– literally *Animal* Garden – was not a mere coincidence. Since the animal dealer and showman Carl Hagenbeck (1844-1913) had developed the concept of ethnographic shows in the 1870s, exhibits of foreign – including African – landscapes, animals, and groups of people were presented to white audiences in Berlin, Basel, Paris, Vienna, Budapest, and other European cities.[8] They satisfied the Europeans' interest in the exotic Other, which was cast as a contrast to the European self-image of civilization and industrialization. This visible presentation of an ostensibly natural polarity between modernity and primitivism contributed to the popularization of pseudo-scientific beliefs justifying the white man's colonial domination over other "races." The traveling villages were usually set up in zoological gardens, which underscored allusions to the projected natural, animal-like primitivism of the human exhibits. In the safe environment of the staged spectacle the shows suggested authentic encounters between European onlookers and foreign "savages."

In Vienna, the first Ashanti exhibit ran from July to October 1896 and caused a veritable "Ashanti fever" among the Viennese, as the show attracted approximately five to six thousand visitors per day. As news-paper articles and the images of bare-breasted Ashanti women in one of Wilhelm Gause's (1853-1916) gouaches attest (fig. 6), the fascination lay as much in the anthropological experience as in the eroticization of the exotic.

Wilhelm Gause's drawings date from 1897 and were presumably made during the second Ashanti exhibit in Vienna in the same year. Although created quite independently of Peter Altenberg's collection of miniature prose also focusing on the Ashanti exhibit, Gause's pieces complement Altenberg's text in as much as they, too, represent, in the realm of graphic art, a white perspective across the cultural and "racial" divide. One of his gouaches (fig. 9) represents the Ashanti's procession through town, another one (fig. 8) introduces the viewer to the general set-up of the artificial Ashanti village in the Vienna Zoological Garden where bourgeois looking, white visitors leisurely stroll around primitive huts and inspect native goods for sale on display tables. A third image (fig. 4) depicts black children orderly seated in an open-air, but fenced-in "school room" under the supervision of a visibly strict African teacher; like animals in a zoo, they are observed by well-dressed white onlookers from outside the fence. Figure 7a captures a white lady's intent, caring and admiring gaze upon an African child. And yet another drawing (fig. 6) shows young African women dancing topless to the drums while a crowd of Africans looks on. The absence of whites in several pictures creates, like the Ashanti characters' direct speech in Altenberg's *Ashantee*, the illusion of an unmediated look into the world and culture of the Ashanti while in actual fact all of Gause's images reflect the gaze and interest of the white painter and his white audience.

Altenberg's literary rendering of the Ashanti exhibit in *Ashantee* and his "sympathetic treatment" of the Ashanti characters have been lauded by literary scholars such as Marilyn Scott, Ian Forster, and Andrew Barker "as an expression of utmost tolerance in the racially-charged atmosphere of the time;" Scott goes so far as to praise the author for "championing the humanity of all races."[9] Dirk Göttsche, David Kim, and Katharina von Hammerstein on the other hand also investigate elements of colonial, hegemonial discourse in Altenberg's representation of Austrian-African encounters.[10] His sketches certainly display genuine curiosity about cultural differences. This is underscored by Altenberg's phonetic rendering of the Ashanti's language[11] as well as the use of several European languages (English and French) in the German-language original. The text demonstrates the best intentions for developing cross-cultural communication and acceptance at a time when accounts of colonial conquest and domination pervaded colonial discourse. It severely criticizes dehumanizing prejudices common among Altenberg's European contemporaries in general and his fellow Viennese in particular. *Ashantee* explicitly exposes the propagandistic function of the pseudo-ethnographic Vienna Ashanti exhibit, which sent a colonial message similar to that of the Paris World Exposition of 1889 when the Eiffel Tower ostensibly proved Western civilization's progress; European "sky-high" superiority would be measured visibly against the exotic "primitivism" of the "savage" Other which was presented as still living in huts and thus as stuck on a lower rung of the evolutionary scale. By contrast, Altenberg's approach is compassionate rather than condescending. In *Ashantee* he has the main character ask Tíoko, one of the young Ashanti women, why she is so scantily dressed on a cold Vienna day; her response introduces the reader to an African perspective: "We are not permitted to wear anything, Sir, no shoes, nothing, we even have to take off the headscarf. ... We are supposed to look like savages, Sir, like Africans. It is completely silly. In Africa we couldn't run around like this. We would be a laughing stock.... Nobody lives in huts like these. In our country, huts are just for dogs, gbè. Quite foolish. They want us to look like animals. What do you think, Sir?!" (36) Altenberg's Jewish background may well have contributed to his sympathy for the colonial underdogs, especially in a political climate in which conservative anti-Semitics likened in derogatory terms the exoticism of the Ashanti to the Otherness of one of Vienna's largest minorities, the Eastern Jews from Galicia.

Comparing Altenberg's *Ashantee* to Rainer Maria Rilke's poem "The Ashanti (Jardin d'Acclimatation)" of 1902[12] which reflects Rilke's impressions of the Ashanti exhibit in Paris, Andrew Barker states, "Whereas Altenberg uses the exploitation of the Ashanti as a basis for a critique of late nineteenth-century mores, Rilke, typically, shies away from the socially critical implications of his material, although they were certainly there, implicitly."[13]

Yet, despite Altenberg's less hidden social criticism and the explicitly "sympathetic treatment" of Africans in his representation of the Ashanti experience, the equally explicit visual and almost tactile quality of it corresponds with the objectifying and eroticizing treatment the Africans, particularly the women, received in the reality of the Zoological Garden where they were, according to newspaper reports, often touched and petted. Altenberg's text is characterized by an inherent white, male gaze[14] – which compares to the onlooker's perspective of Wilhelm Gause's gouaches – and by frequent physical contact between the author's literary double Sir Peter and young Ashanti women and girls. He frequently embraces and kisses them, his eyes seem to caress their "wonderful light brown breasts" (34), their "skin like silk" (45) and "blossoming body" (46), and he is eventually portrayed as stepping out of Akolé's hut "in first light of dawn" (57) – an allusion to the mediaeval literary genre of *Tagelied* (dawn song) which captures two lovers' parting after a night of passion. While well-meaning and presented in the light of protective paternalism, the character's gaze and touch seem to invade the African women's naked bodies in a fashion similar to contemporary colonialists around the world who invaded defenseless geographical borders and appropriated foreign territories. Susanne Zantop comments on this phenomenon: "Ironically, it [the desire to appropriate foreign territories] often appeared under the guise of an anticolonialist stance. Indeed, the drive for colonial possession – and by this I mean actual control over territories and resources as well as control over the body and labor of human beings – articulated itself not so much in statements of intent as in 'colonial fantasies': stories of sexual conquest and surrender, love and blissful domestic relations between colonizer and colonized."[15] While situated in Vienna and not in the colonies, Altenberg's *Ashantee* nevertheless reflects these "colonial fantasies" of harmonious and erotic relations between Europeans and Africans. The text's construction of the African woman as a beautiful, sensual, childlike, emotional, natural, and wholesome female Other who provides inspiration for the tormented civilized soul of the male Self, is furthermore reminiscent of both the German Romantics' essentializing construction of woman as the fragmented man's harmonious savior and of the primitivist discourse which is, according to Marianna Torgovnick, "fundamental to the Western sense of Self and Other."[16]

Despite Peter Altenberg's apparent awareness that concepts of "race" and primitivism are cultural and scientifically theoretical constructs, the literary rendering of his enthusiastic communication and mutual friendship with the African "paradise people" (27), as he calls them in his dedication, bears elements of an idealizing projection. The text's ambivalence, between integrative cross-cultural sympathy on the one hand and differentiating colonialist stereotyping on the other, becomes particularly obvious when the main character states, "Negroes are children.... Negroes are just like sweet, silent nature. They strike a chord in you, while they themselves are without music.... They are ... the conductors of our symphony orchestra. They themselves don't play an instrument, they conduct our soul" (51). Altenberg's text thereby advocates what Torgovnick identifies as one of the tropes of primitivist discourse: "Primitives are like children, the tropes say. Primitives are our untamed selves, our id force.... Primitives are mystics, in tune with nature, part of its harmonies. Primitives are free. Primitives exist on the 'lowest cultural levels'; we occupy the 'highest.'"[17]

Thus, Altenberg's romanticization of the African Other as "purer," more genuine[18] and less affected than Europeans, more specifically Austrians, centers not on the Other, but on the Self. It implies an essentializing differentiation between the "cultured" Europeans and "natural and childlike" non-Europeans. More importantly, it reflects a lack of sincere concern for the predicaments the real, non-fictional Ashanti face in Europe and West Africa. The text makes little mention of the uneven power relations between Austrians and Ashanti and none of the military struggle the Ashanti faced with the British colonial power which humiliated and exiled the ruler of Asante in 1896[19] – the very year Altenberg met the troupe in Vienna.

Reveling in the illusion that empathy alone could abolish differences of culture and interest between Europeans and Africans, Altenberg and his character Sir Peter remain essentially tied to their own cultural and mental environment, captive to the colonial structure the work sets out to attack. Despite the work's title *Ashantee*, the African Other seems relevant only as an impression on and a projection of the European, specifically Austrian, Self. Despite the text's obvious attempt to promote cross-cultural integration and despite its explicit criticism of racial and colonial prejudices, the binaries of colonial discourse – Self vs. Other, culture vs. nature, mind vs. body, male vs. female, subject vs. object, familiar vs. exotic, European vs. non-European, power vs. powerlessness – remain in place, even if Altenberg inverts the hierarchy of low vs. high on the evolutionary scale to spite his fellow Viennese.

The contradictions we find in *Ashantee* are symptomatic of the political climate in Europe around 1900 that saw anticolonialist sentiments and critique of civilization side by side with colonialist discourse. The racist and sexist elements in Altenberg's *Ashantee* (despite the author's declared admiration of the African "paradise people") and the work's Eurocentric perspective of encounters with the African Other were in themselves not unusual in the colonial era. In fact, such elements were common even among liberals, including Pablo Picasso (1881-1973) in France (e.g., reflected in his famous 1907 painting "Les Desmoiselles d'Avignon") and several German Expressionist painters (e.g., Max Pechstein 1881-1955 and Irma Stern 1894-1966). They greatly admired African art and projected a mentality onto this African Other which they perceived as unspoiled by civilization.[20] The very enthusiasm for Blackness in *Ashantee* is an example of how "even anticolonially motivated texts ... reproduce the essentialization of Self and Other that was so characteristic of colonial discourse."[21]

Notes

[1] Max Messer. "Peter Altenberg und sein neues Buch 'Ashantee,'" *Wiener Rundschau* 2.14 (1. Juni 1897): 543.

[2] The term "race" has become questionable in modern science and discourse. It is used here to signify not a biological category, but a social construct.

[3] Mary Louise Pratt, "Arts of the Contact Zone," *Profession* 91, repr. *Ways of Reading: An Anthology for Writers*, David Bartholomae and Anthony Petrosky (eds.), Boston: St. Martin's Press, 1999, 584.

[4] While Austria-Hungary was not successful in obtaining any colonies, it nevertheless condoned and supported European colonialism through foreign policy and scientific excursions and actively participated in the colonial discourse. See the publications by Johannes Feichtinger et al., Wolfgang Müller-Funk et al., and Walter Sauer in the attached bibliography.

[5] In the late nineteenth century, the Habsburg Empire included land and peoples from what today would be Austria, Southern Poland, Slovakia, Czech Republic, Hungary, Slovenia, Croatia, Bosnia, Herzegovina, Serbia, and Northern Italy.

[6] See the publications by Katharina von Hammerstein listed in the attached bibliography.

[7] For information about the Ashanti exhibits in Vienna, see the publications by Peter Plener and Werner Michael Schwarz listed in the attached bibliography.

[8] For information about ethnographic exhibits (Völkerschauen) in Europe in general, see the publications by Eric Ames, Rea Brändle, Stefan Goldmann, Carl Hagenbeck, Alexander Honold, Bernth Lindfors, Werner Michael Schwarz, Baltasahr Staehelin, and Hilke Thode-Arora listed in the attached bibliography.

[9] Marilyn Scott, "A Zoo Story: Peter Altenberg's *Ashantee* (1897)," *Modern Austrian Literature* 30.2 (July 1997): 51 and 59.

[10] For scholarship on Altenberg's *Ashantee*, see the publications by the scholars mentioned here as well as those by Lisa Gates, Sander Gilman (specifically "Black Sexuality and Modern Consciousness"), Angelika Jacobs, Heinz Lunzer et al., and Uta Sadji, all listed in the attached bibliography.

[11] The examples of Ghanaian language which Altenberg calls "Odji" are, in fact, from one of the Dangme languages spoken in Ghana. For Altenberg's poetic interplay with languages as a medium of negotiation between Self and Other, see David Kim's publication listed in the attached bibliography.

[12] Rainer Maria Rilke, "Die Aschanti (Jardin d'Acclimatation)," *Werke in drei Bänden*, Beda Allemann (ed.),

Frankfurt/M.: Insel, 1966, 1:150-51, translated by Andrew Barker in: Andrew W. Barker, "Unforgettable People From Paradise: Peter Altenberg and the Ashanti visit to Vienna of 1896-97," *Research in African Literatures* 22.2 (Summer 1991): 66.

[13] Ibid.

[14] For "modernism's two powerful objectifying gazes – those of patriarchy, the much-debated 'male gaze,' and of colonialism – the 'imperial gaze,'" see Ann Kaplan, *Looking for the Other: Feminism, Film, and the Imperial Gaze*. New York and London: Routledge, 1997, 22.

[15] Susanne Zantop, *Colonial Fantasies. Conquest, Family, and Nation in Precolonial Germany, 1770-1870*, Durham and London: Duke University Press, 1997, 2.

[16] Marianna Torgovnick, *Gone Primitive: Savage Intellects, Modern Lives*, Chicago/London: University of Chicago Press, 1990, 8.

[17] Ibid.

[18] Altenberg describes the real-life Ashanti in a letter as "naked, wonderfully developed, free people with a sense of peace" (to Annie Holitscher, August 11, 1896, cit. Hans Christian Kosler (ed.), *Peter Altenberg. Leben und Werk in Texten und Bildern*, München: Matthes & Seitz, 1981, 165, my translation.

[19] For information about the history of Asante and the Ashanti, see the publications by Thomas Lewin, T.C. McCaskie, Robert Rattray, Ivor Wilks listed in the attached bibliography.

[20] See Jost Hermand, "Artificial Atavism: German Expressionism and Blacks," Reinhold Grimm and Jost Hermand (eds.), *Blacks in German Culture*, Madison: University of Wisconsin Press, 1986, 65-86.

[21] Sebastian Connrad and Shalini Randeria (eds.), *Jenseits des Eurozentrismus. Postkoloniale Perspektiven in den Ge-schichts- und Kulturwissenschaften*, Frankfurt/M./New York: Campus, 2002, 35.

Editor's and Translator's Note

This edition is based on Peter Altenberg's first edition of *Ashantee* (Berlin: Samuel Fischer Publishers, 1897). It includes five additional sections inserted by the author in 1904 when *Ashantee* appeared as part of the forth edition of Altenberg's *Wie ich es sehe* (How I See It; Berlin: Samuel Fischer Publishers, 1904): "Adultry" (Ehebruch); "Beatings" (Prügel); "Dowry" (Mitgift); "Hereditary Succession" (Erbfolge); and "Motherhood" (Mütterlichkeit). Not reflected in this edition are the slight changes in "Chivalry" (Ritterlichkeit) and the omission of ten original sections in the 1904 edition: "Conversation" (Gespräch); Multiplication Tables (Einmaleins); "The Huts (In the Evening)" (Die Hütten [Abends]); "Dinner" (Souper); "Akolé;" "A Letter from Vienna (To the Negro Woman Monambô)" (Ein Brief aus Wien [An die Negerin Monambô]); "Translation of 'A Letter from Vienna'" (Übersetzung von 'Ein Brief aus Wien'); "Le Coeur;" "Conclusion;" "Le Depart Pour l'Afrique."

This translation stays close to Altenberg's original style and follows his original punctuation. The edition maintains Altenberg's irregular spelling of Ashanti names as well as his phonetic rendering of the Ashanti's language. The footnotes were added by the editor.

I thank Jorun Johns for having accompanied this project to completion and Wolfgang Nehring for his very thoughtful introduction. I am much indebted to Ritta Jo Horsley, Edward Shaw, and Damon Guizot for their native-tongue input to my translating this volume and to Oliver Hiob for his help with the intricacies of technology. And finally, I am grateful to my husband Jacques Govignon for his encouraging, never ceasing support.

Selected Bibliography

Peter Altenberg's *Ashantee*,
Asante,
Vienna around 1900,
Ethnographic Exhibits of
Africans in Europe,
Postcolonial Theory

Agbodeka, Francis. *African Politics and British Policy in the Gold Coast 1868-1900: A Study in the Forms and Force of Protest.* Evanston, IL: Northwestern University Press, 1971.

Ames, Eric. "Animal Attractions: Cinema, Exoticism, and German Modernity." *Österreichische Zeitschrift für Geschichtswissenschaften* 12.1 (2001): 7-14.

Ames. Eric. *Where the Wild Things are. Locating the Exotic in German Modernity.* Diss. University of California, Berkeley, 2000.

"Ausstellung im Jüdischen Museum: Peter Altenberg. extracte des lebens." Kuratoren Heinz Lunzer, Victoria Lunzer-Talos, Marcus G. Patka. Jüdisches Museum, Wien, 22. Jänner bis 27. April 2003. www.literaturhaus.at/autoren/Alltenberg/ausstellung juedisch/

Badenberg, Nana. "Mohrenwäsche, Völkerschauen: Der Konsum des Schwarzen um 1900." Ed. Birgit Tautz. *Colors 1800/1900/2000: Signs of Ethnic Difference.* Amsterdam, New York/NY: Rodopi, 2004. 163-184.

Barker, Andrew. "Peter Altenberg." *Dictionary of Literary Biography.* Vol. 81, Austrian Fiction Writers, 1875-1913. Ed. James Hardin and Donald G. Gaviau. Detroit, Michigan: Gale Research Inc., 1989. 81:3-10.

Barker, Andrew W. "Franz Kafka and Peter Altenberg." Ed. Jeffrey B. Berlin, Jorun B. Johns, and Richard H. Lawson. *Turn-of-the-Century Vienna and Its Legacy. Essays in Honor of Donald G. Daviau.* Wien: Edition Atelier, 1993. 221-238.

Barker, Andrew W. "'Ein Lichtbringender und Leuchtender, ein Dichter und Prophet': Responses to Peter Altenberg in Turn-of-the-Century Vienna." *Modern Austrian Literature* 22.3/4 (1989): 1-14.

Barker, Andrew. *Telegrams from the Soul: Peter Altenberg and the Culture of Fin-de-siècle Vienna.* Columbia, SC: Camden House, 1996.

Barker, Andrew W. "Unforgettable People from Paradise: Peter Altenberg and the Ashanti Visit to Vienna of 1896-97." *Research in African Literatures* 22.2 (Summer 1991): 55-70.

Barker, Andrew and Leo A. Lensing. *Peter Altenberg: Rezept die Welt zu sehen.* Wien: Braumüller, 1995.

Bechhaus-Gerst, Marianne and Reinhard Klein-Arendt (eds.). *AfrikanerInnen in Deutschland und schwarze Deutsche – Geschichte und Gegenwart. Beiträge zur gleichnamigen Konferenz vom 13.-15. Juni 2003 im NS-Dokumentationszentrum Köln.* Münster: LIT, 2004.

Bechhaus-Gerst, Marianne and Reinhard Klein-Arndt (eds). *Die (koloniale) Begegnung: AfrikanerInnen in Deutschland 1880-1945 – Deutsche in Afrika 1880-1980.* Frankfurt/M./New York: Peter Lang, 2003.

Beller, Steven (ed.). *Rethinking Vienna 1900.* Oxford/New York: Berghahn Books, 2001.

Berman, Russell A. *Enlightenment or Empire. Colonial Discourse in German Culture.* Lincoln & London: University of Nebraska Press, 1998.

Bisanz, Hans. *Peter Altenberg. Mein äußerstes Ideal. Altenbergs Photosammlung von geliebten Frauen, Freunden und Orten.* Wien-München: Verlag Christian Brandstätter, 1984.

Bowdich, T. Edward. *Mission From Cape Coast Castle To Ashantee* 1824. Ed. W.E.F. Ward. 3rd ed. Brussels/ Belgium: Frank Cass & Co., 1966.

Brändle, Rea. *Wildfremd, hautnah. Völkerschauen und Schauplätze. Zürich 1880-1960. Bilder und Geschichten.* Zürich: Rotpunktverlag, 1995.

Conrad, Sebastian and Shalini Randeria (eds.). *Jenseits des Eurozentrismus. Postkoloniale Perspektiven in den Geschichts- und Kulturwissenschaften.* Frankfurt/M./New York: Campus, 2002.

de Rider, Jacques and Rosemary Morris. *Modernity and Crisis of Identity: Culture and Society in Fin-de-siècle Vienna.* Oxford: Blackwell Publishers, 1993.

Dunker, Axel (ed.). *(Post-)Kolonialismus und deutsche Literatur. Impulse der angloamerikanischen Literatur- und Kulturtheorie.* Bielefeld: Aisthesis, 2005.

Feichtinger, Johannes, Ursula Prutsch and Moritz Csaky (eds.). *Habsburg postcolonial: Machtstrukturen und kollektives Gedächtnis.* Innsbruck: Studienverlag, 2003.

Foster, Ian. "Altenberg's African Spectacle: *Ashantee* in Context." Ed. Ritchie Robertson and Edward Timms. *Theatre and Performance in Austria: From Mozart to Jelinek.* Edinburgh: Edinburgh University Press, 1993. 39-60.

Foster, Ian. "Peter Altenberg und das Fremde." Ed. Anne Fuchs and Theo Harden. *Reisen im Diskurs. Modelle der literarischen Fremderfahrung von den Pilgerberichten bis zur Postmoderne.* Heidelberg: Universitätsverlag C. Winter, 1995. 333-342.

Friedell, Egon (ed.). *Das Altenbergbuch.* Leipzig/Wien: Wiener Graphische Werkstätte, 1922.

Friedell, Egon. *Ecce Poeta.* Zürich: Diogenes, 1992.

Friedell, Egon. "Egon Friedell über Peter Altenberg." Friedell, Egon. *Kulturgeschichte der Neuzeit.* München: H.C. Beck, 1984. 1456-1458. Reprint: http://ourworld.compuserve.com/homepages/ulrich _oswald.friedell.htm

Friedrichsmeyer, Sara, Sara Lennox, and Susanne Zantop (eds.). *The Imperialist Imagination: German Colonialism and Its Legacy.* Ann Arbor: University of Michigan Press, 1998.

Gates, Lisa Marie. *Images of Africa in Late Nineteenth and Twentieth-Century German Literature and Culture.* Ann Arbor: University of Michigan Press, 2002.

Gilman, Sander. "Black Bodies, White Bodies: Toward an Iconography of Female Sexuality in Late Nineteenth-Century Art, Medicine, and Literature." Ed. Henry Louis Gates Jr. *"Race," Writing and Difference.* Chicago/ London: University of Chicago Press, 1985. 223-261.

Gilman, Sander. "Black Sexuality and Modern Consciousness." Ed. Reinhold Grimm and Jost Hermand. *Blacks and German Culture.* Madison: University of Wisconsin Press, 1986. 35-53.

Gilman, Sander L. *On Blackness without Blacks: Essays on the Image of the Black in Germany.* Boston: G.K. Hall, 1982.

Gilman, Sander. *Difference and Pathology: Stereotypes of Sexuality, Race and Madness*. Ithaca/NY: Cornell University Press, 1985.

Gilman, Sander L. "The Image of the Black in the German Colonial Novel." Ed. Sander Gilman. *On Blackness without Blacks: Essays on the Image of the Black in Germany*. Boston: G.K. Hall, 1982. 119-155.

Gilman, Sander. "The Figure of the Black in German Aesthetic Theory." *Eighteenth-Century Studies* 8 (1975): 373-391.

Goldmann, Stefan. "Wilde in Europa. Aspekte und Orte ihrer Zurschaustellung." Ed. Thomas Theye. *Wir und die Wilden. Einblicke in eine kannibalische Beziehung*. Reinbeck: Rowohlt, 1985. 243-269.

Goldmann, Stefan. "Zur Rezeption der Völkerausstellungen um 1900." Ed. Hermann Pollig et al. *Exotische Welten. Europäische Phantasien*. Stuttgart: Cantz 1987. 88-95.

Göttsche, Dirk. "Kolonialismus und Interkulturalität in Peter Altenbergs 'Ashantee'-Skizzen." Ed. Axel Dunker. *(Post-)Kolonialismus und deutsche Literatur. Impulse der angloamerikanischen Literatur- und Kulturtheorie*. Bielefeld: Aisthesis 2005. 161-178.

Grabovszki, Ernst and James Hardin (eds.). *Literature in Vienna at the Turn of the Centuries: Continuities and Discontinuities around 1900 and 2000*. Rochester: Camden House, 2002.

Grimm, Reinhold and Jost Hermand (eds.). *Blacks in German Culture*. Madison: University of Wisconsin Press, 1986.

Hagenbeck, Carl. *Von Tieren und Menschen. Erlebnisse und Erfahrungen.* Berlin: Vita Deutsches Verlagshaus, 1908.

Hammerstein, Katharina von. "Looking B(l)ack: Inter-Gender and Interracial Gaze in European and African Represenations Around 1900." Ed. Elke Frederiksen. *Within Global Contexts: Literature and Culture of German-Speaking Europe.* Oxford, New York: Berghahn. Forthcoming.

Hammerstein, Katharina von. "Challenges of Cross-Cultural Dialog: The African Other in Peter Altenberg's *Ashantee* (1897)." *Teaching Austria* 1 (2005): 1-22, and 22 PowerPoint slides. http://www.malca.org/ta/v1/vol1.html.

Hammerstein, Katharina von. "'Dem edlen Männer-Auge ein Bild ...' Ambivalenz der anti/kolonialen Repräsentation in Peter Altenbergs *Ashantee.*" *Konstruktionen von Afrika(nerInnen) in der deutschen Kultur.* Ed. Marianne Bechhaus-Gerst and Sunna Gieseke. Frankfurt/M./Zürich/New York: Peter Lang, 2006. 131-142.

Hammerstein, Katharina von. "'Neger sind Kinder.' Wohlwollender Essentialismus in Peter Altenbergs *Ashantee.*" *Jahrbuch für internationale Germanistik* 85. Forthcoming.

Hammerstein, Katharina von. "Utopian Visions of 'Universal Sympathy': Self-Centered Cross-Culturalism in Peter Altenberg's *Ashantee* (1897)." *International Journal of the Humanities* 2.2 (2004-2006): 1121-1129.

Hermand, Jost. "Artificial Atavism: German Expressionism and Blacks." Ed. Reinhold Grimm and

Jost Hermand. *Blacks in German Culture*. Madison: University of Wisconsin Press, 1986. 65-86.

Hofmannsthal, Hugo von. "Ein neues Wiener Buch." *Gesammelte Werke, Reden und Aufsätze I*. Ed. Bernd Schoeller. Frankfurt/M.: Fischer, 1979. 222-230.

Honold, Alexander. "Ausstellung des Fremden – Menschen- und Völkerschau um 1900. Zwischen Anpassung und Verfremdung: Der Exot und sein Publikum." Ed. Sebastian Conrad and Jürgen Osterhammel. *Das Kaiserreich transnational. Deutschland in der Welt 1871-1914*. Göttingen: Vandenhoeck & Ruprecht, 2004. 170-190.

Höpp, Gerhard (ed.). *Fremde Erfahrung. Asiaten und Afrikaner in Deutschland, Österreich und in der Schweiz bis 1945*. Berlin: Verlag Das Arabische Buch, 1996.

Jacobs, Angelika. "'Wildnis' als Wunschtraum westlicher 'Zivilisation': Zur Kritik des Exotismus in Peter Altenbergs *Ashantee* und Robert Müllers *Tropen*." *Germanica: Jahrbuch für deutschlandkundliche Studien* 8 (2001), reprinted in: http://www.kakanien.ac.at/beitr/fallstudie/AJacobs1. pdf

Kaplan, Ann: *Looking for the Other: Feminism, Film, and the Imperial Gaze*. New York and London: Routledge, 1997.

Kim, David D. "The Task of the Loving Translator: Translation, *Völkerschauen*, and Colonial Ambivalence in Peter Altenberg's *Ashantee* (1897)." *TRANSIT* 2.1 (2006), Article 60404. http://repositories.cdlib.org/ucbgerman/transit/vol2 /iss1/art60404

Köwer, Irene. *Peter Altenberg als Autor der literarischen Kleinform. Untersuchungen zu seinem Werk unter gattungstypologischem Aspekt.* Frankfurt/M.: Lang, 1987.

Kopp, Kristin und Klaus Müller-Richter (eds.). *Die 'Großstadt' und das 'Primitive'. Text–Politik–Repräsentation.* Stuttgart: Metzler, 2004.

Kosler, Hans Christian (ed.). *Peter Altenberg. Leben und Werk in Texten und Bildern.* München: Matthes & Seitz, 1981.

Kraus, Karl. "Rede am Grabe Peter Altenbergs, 11. Juni 1919." *Die Fackel* 508 (1919): 8-25.

Lensing, Leo. "Peter Altenbergs 'beschriebene' Photographien: Ein zweites Oeuvre?" *Foto-geschichte.* 15.57 (1995): 3-33.

Lindfors, Bernth (ed.). *Africans on Stage. Studies in Ethnological Show Business.* Bloomington, IN: Indiana University Press, 1999.

Lindfors, Bernth. "Hottentotten, Bushman, Kaffir: The Making of Racist Stereotypes in 19th-Century Britain." Ed. Mai Palmberg. *Encounter Images in the Meeting between Africa and Europe.* Uppsala/Sweden: Nordiska Afrikainstitutet, 2001. 54-74.

Lunzer, Heinz et al. (eds). *Peter Altenberg. Extracte des Lebens. Einem Schriftsteller auf der Spur.* Salzburg/Vienna: Residenzverlag, 2003.

Messer, Max. "Peter Altenberg und sein neues Buch 'Ashantee.'" *Wiener Rundschau* 2.14 (1. Juni 1897): 540-543.

McCaskie, T.C. *Asante Identities: History and Modernity in an African Village 1850-1950*. London: Edinburgh University Press and Bloomington: Indiana University Press: 2000.

Müller-Funk, Wolfgang, Peter Plener, and Clemens Ruthner. *Kakanien revisited: Das Eigene und das Fremde (in) der österreich-ungarischen Monarchie*. Tübingen: Francke, 2002.

Oguntoye, Katharina, May Opitz, and Dagmar Schultz (eds.). *Farbe bekennen: Afro-deutsche Frauen auf den Spuren ihrer Geschichte*. Berlin: Orlanda, 1986. Transl. by Anne V. Adams as *Showing Our Colors: Afro-German Women Speak Out*. Amherst, MA: University of Massachusetts Press, 1992.

Palmberg, Mai (ed.). *Encounter Images in the Meeting between Africa and Europe*. Uppsala/Sweden: Nordiska Afrika-institutet, 2001.

"Peter Altenberg." *Lexikon: Literatur in der Wiener Moderne*. www.sbg.ac.at/lwm/frei/genetated/a39.html

Plener, Peter. "(K)Ein Mohr im Hemd: Aschantis in Budapest und Wien, 1896/97." *Kakanien Revisited* (06/11/2001): 1-4.

Pratt, Mary Louise. "Arts of the Contact Zone." *Profession* 91. Repr. *Ways of Reading: An Anthology for Writers*. Ed. David Bartholomae and Anthony Petrosky. Boston: St. Martin's Press, 1999. 582-600.

Pratt, Mary Louise. *Imperial Eyes. Travel Writing and Transculturalism*. New York: Routledge, 1992.

Rattray, Robert: *Ashanti.* Oxford: Clarendon Press, 1923.

"Richard Engländer alias Peter Altenberg, 1859-1919."
www.werbeka.com/ffha/ab.htm

Rilke, Rainer Maria. "Die Aschanti (Jardin d'Acclimatation)." *Werke in drei Bänden.* Ed. Beda Allemann.
Frankfurt/M.: Insel, 1966, 1:150-151.

Sadji, Uta. "Sage mir was der Wald ist, das Kind, der
Neger. Peter Altenbergs *Ashantee*-Episode." *Études
Germano-Africaines: Revue Annuelle de Germaniques
Africaine* 11 (1993): 146-153.

Sauer, Walter (ed.). *Das afrikanische Wien. Ein Führer zu
Bieber, Malangatana, Soliman.* Wien: SADOCC, 1996.

Sauer, Walter (ed.). *k. u. k. kolonial. Habsburgermonarchie und
europäische Herrschaft in Afrika.* Wien, Köln, Weimar:
Böhlau, 2002.

Schoenberg, Barbara Zeisl. "How 'Belle' Was the 'Belle
Époque' Really? Some Not So 'Belle' Reflections of
Vienna in the 'Belle Époque.' Mirrors of Kraus,
Altenberg and Petzold." *Austria in Literature.* Ed.
Donald G. Daviau. Riverside, CA: Ariadne Press,
2000. 60-74.

Schorske, Carl E. *Fin-De-Siècle Vienna: Politics and Culture.*
New York: Vintage, 1980.

Schwarz, Thomas. "Colonialism and Exoticism: A Special
Evolution of German Literature?" Ed. Theo D'Haen
and Patricia Krüs. *Colonizer and Colonized.*
Amsterdam/Atlanta: Rodopi, 2000. 565-576.

Schwarz, Werner Michael. *Anthropologische Spektakel. Zur*

126

Schaustellung "exotischer" Menschen, Wien 1870-1910. Wien: Turia + Kant, 2001.

Schwarz, Werner Michael (ed.). *Ashantee. Afrika und Wien um die Jahrhundertwende.* Wien: Löcker, 2007.

Schwarz, Werner Michael. "Echte und falsche Menschen. 'Anthropologisches Spektakel' in Wien." Ed. Kristin Kopp und Klaus Müller-Richter (eds.). *Die 'Großstadt' und das 'Primitive'. Text–Politik–Repräsentation.* Stuttgart: Metzler, 2004. 53-67.

Schwarz, Werner Michael. "Konsum des Anderen. Schaustellung exotischer Menschen in Wien." *Österreichische Zeitschrift für Geschichtswissenschaften* 12.1 (2001): 15-29.

Scott, Marilyn. "A Zoo Story: Peter Altenberg's *Ashantee* (1897)." *Modern Austrian Literature* 30.2 (July 1997): 48-64.

Staehelin, Baltasahr. *Völkerschauen im Zoologischen Garten Basel 1879-1935.* Basel: Basler Afrika Bibliographien, 1993.

Stein, Martin. *Das Bild des Schwarzen in der europäischen Kolonialliteratur 1870-1918: Ein Beitrag zur literarischen Imagologie.* Frankfurt/M.: Thesen-Verlag, 1972.

Tautz, Birgit (ed.). *Colors 1800 / 1900 / 2000. Signs of Ethnic Difference.* Amsterdam/New York, NY: Amsterdamer Beiträge, 2004.

Thode-Arora, Hilke. *Für fünfzig Pfennig um die Welt. Die Hagenbeck'schen Völkerschauen.* Frankfurt/M./New York: Campus, 1989.

Thode-Arora. Hilke. "Afrika-Völkerschauen in Deutsch-land." Ed. Marianne Bechhaus-Gerst and Reinhard Klein-Arendt. *AfrikanerInnen in Deutschland und schwarze Deutsche–Geschichte und Gegenwart. Beiträge zur gleich-namigen Konferenz vom 13.-15. Juni 2003 im NS-Dokumentationszentrum Köln.* Münster: LIT, 2004. 25-40.

Torgovnick, Marianna. *Gone Primitive: Savage Intellects, Modern Lives.* Chicago/London: University of Chicago Press, 1990.

van der Heyden, Ulrich. *Die Begegnung mit dem Fremden in Europa.* Stuttgart: Institut für Auslandsbeziehungen, 1998.

Vera, Yvonne. "A Voyeur's Paradise... Images of Africa." Ed. Mai Palmberg. *Encounter Images in the Meeting between Africa and Europe.* Uppsala/Sweden: Nordiska Afrika-institutet, 2001. 115-120.

Wilks, Ivor. *Forests of Gold. Essays on the Akan and the Kingdom of Asante.* Athens: Ohio University Press, 1993.

Wilks, Ivor. *Asante in the Nineteenth Century: The Structure and Evolution of a Political Order.* London/New York: Cambridge University Press: 1975.

Wunberg, Gotthart (ed.). *Das junge Wien. Österreichische Literatur- und Kunstkritik.* 2 vols., vol. 1. Tübingen: Niemeyer, 1976.

Young, Robert J.C. *Colonial Desire: Hybridity in Theory, Culture and Race.* London/New York: Routledge, 1995.

Young, Robert. *White Mythologies: Writing History and the West.* London: Routledge, 1990.

Zantop, Susanne: *Colonial Fantasies. Conquest, Family, and Nation in Precolonial Germany, 1770-1870*. Durham: London: Duke University Press, 1997. Transl. as *Kolonialphantasien im vorkolonialen Deutschland (1770-1870)*. Berlin: Erich Schmidt, 1999.

This collection of thirty-eight impressionist episodes describes a white man's friendship with a group of Ashanti tribespeople from the Gold Coast of Africa (the former British colony known today as Ghana) who in 1896 were put on display as living objects in a popular ethnographic exhibit in the Vienna Zoological Garden, then still located in Vienna's park called Prater. The exhibit caused a veritable "Ashanti fever" as it attracted five to six thousand visitors per day. Altenberg, barely disguised as *Ashantee's* autobiographical character Sir Peter, shows a genuine curiosity about the cultural Other and paints a critical picture of his Austrian contemporaries' prejudices, revealed as they were experienced by the Africans. In *Ashantee,* beautiful, sensual, childlike, and wholesome African "paradise people" provide inspiration for the tormented civilized soul of the *fin-de-siècle* European. Eccentric coffeehouse writer Altenberg is famous for his unique telegram style. Critic Karl Kraus claimed, "One sentence by Peter Altenberg is equal to an entire Viennese novel."

Ashantee introduces the reader to a little known facet of vibrant Vienna around 1900. Considering the contemporary challenges of cultural coexistence in the global society, the book merits new popularity because of its relevance today as an illustration of encounters between people of different ethnic and cultural backgrounds.

In this edition, Peter Altenberg's literary text is illustrated with reprints of original drawings and photographs of Altenberg and the Ashanti in Vienna.

CPSIA information can be obtained at www.ICGtesting.com
Printed in the USA
LVOW121214190212

269376LV00001B/8/P